Anonymous

Memorial Of The Most Reverend Michael Augustine Corrigan D. D.

Third Archbishop of New York

Anonymous

Memorial Of The Most Reverend Michael Augustine Corrigan D. D.
Third Archbishop of New York

ISBN/EAN: 9783744653381

Printed in Europe, USA, Canada, Australia, Japan

Cover: Foto ©Raphael Reischuk / pixelio.de

More available books at **www.hansebooks.com**

MEMORIAL

OF

THE MOST REVEREND
MICHAEL AUGUSTINE CORRIGAN
D. D.

THIRD ARCHBISHOP OF NEW YORK

✠

COMPILED AND PUBLISHED
BY AUTHORITY

NEW YORK
THE CATHEDRAL LIBRARY ASSOCIATION
1902

CONTENTS

LIST OF ILLUSTRATIONS

ix

PREFACE

THE publication of the present volume is a duty owed to the memory of our dead Archbishop. His character and his office were so blended in him in life as to make him an exemplar of all the qualities required in a prelate of the Church. The realization of this truth was so marked and so general that, when the unexpected intelligence came that he had laid down forever his life's work, a shock and a sorrow went through the community in every class and condition of its people. The memorable fact was then witnessed of not only the great city of his labors, but also the whole country of his birth, being stirred in such a way as to shut out thought of any other event which, under other circumstances, would be of surpassing interest. In spite of his own lifelong modesty and reserve, it was then clearly seen that he was the foremost figure in the respect and affection of his fellow-citizens.

His unassuming personality and his gentle methods, his considerate kindness, and his unaffected piety were the pathways to the love and veneration of his own flock.

His steadfast adherence to principle as well as his persuasive manner of not only teaching, but also of acting out the doctrines of his religion, won for him a high and unique place in the esteem of those who rejoiced in his friendship or acquaintance.

His profound scholarship and his experienced judgment, and withal his unselfish devotion, were ever, when there was question of a religious, moral, or civil import, at the service of his fellow-men.

The testimony to the truth of all that is here said is contained in the following pages. They comprise the sentiments of the Holy Father himself, the thoughts and feelings of high civil dignitaries of the land, of his brethren in the episcopate, of his own stricken clergy and laity on the mournful occasion of his decease.

Moreover, how the nation at large was affected by the sad event, the notices herein reproduced from the public press abundantly bear witness.

The purpose of the present volume, then, is, in the first place, to preserve valuable matter for the future historian of the Church in America, and, in the second place, to give expression to the deep sense of gratitude that wells up in the hearts of so many for having been the favored beneficiaries of the wise rule and the patient kindness, of the noble manhood and the saintly career, of the third of New York's illustrious archbishops, Michael A. Corrigan.

JOSEPH F. MOONEY, V.G.

A BIOGRAPHICAL SKETCH

THE
MOST REV. MICHAEL AUGUSTINE CORRIGAN, D.D.

A BIOGRAPHICAL SKETCH

BORN on the thirteenth day of August, 1839, in Market Street, near Broad, Newark, New Jersey, Michael Augustine, son of Thomas and Mary Corrigan, received the sacrament of Baptism at the home of his parents on the fifteenth of the following month. Of nine children, eight of whom were boys, Michael Augustine was the fifth child and the fourth boy. A native of Kells, County Meath, Ireland, his father, Thomas, son of Philip Corrigan and of Anne Carroll, emigrating in 1828, at the age of twenty-nine, settled in Newark, where for a time he followed the trade of a cabinet-maker—a trade in which he had served an indentured apprenticeship in Dublin. Mary, the mother of Michael Augustine, was one of six children, the offspring of Eleanor Hoey and of Thomas English, of Kingscourt, in the County of Cavan. The Hoeys were Catholics, while the Englishes were Presbyterians; a brother of Thomas being a minister of that denomination. After the death of Thomas English, who, possessing a large tract of land under an interminable lease, left his widow in comfortable circumstances, Eleanor Hoey English, with her children, followed two brothers and two sisters, in 1827, and took up a residence in Brooklyn, Long Island. From Brooklyn she removed to Newark, where, on the thirty-first day of July, 1831, her daughter, Mary English, married Thomas Corrigan.

Fairly well educated for their day, father and mother were gifted with that love of learning which, implanted by nature in the soul of their race, has, through all the centuries of trial, been nurtured by the traditions of a famous past, if not by the hope of a more famous future. Before 1850 there was no parochial school in Newark, nor were there any other public schools to boast of. However, at least one scholarly teacher had been tempted to seek a livelihood in Newark—Bernard Kearney, a native of Malahide, near Dublin; the son of a schoolmaster who had himself made thorough studies in an ecclesiastical seminary. Facing many discouragements, Bernard Kearney slowly earned a reputation for ability, and his private school, in Plane Street, attracted Protestant as well as Catholic youth. Under him, Michael Augustine, who, by the way, was the godson of his tutor, beginning in 1848, made his preparatory studies in the English branches, in mathematics, and in Latin also. At the Sunday-school of St. John's Church—a school organized by the priest who baptized him, and the first Sunday-school in New Jersey—he was a pupil under Father Patrick Moran, one of the pioneers; and of this church he was an acolyte, as, later, he was of St. Patrick's, the present Cathedral, where, on the fourteenth of September, 1851, he first received the Holy Communion.

At the age of fourteen his parents sent him to St. Mary's College, Wilmington, Delaware. There he passed the two scholastic years 1853–55. On March 5, 1854, in St. Peter's Church, Wilmington, the sacrament of Confirmation was administered to him by the saintly Bishop John Neumann of Philadelphia. From St. Mary's, Wilmington, he went to

Michael A. Corrigan
Mount St. Mary's College

Michael A. Corrigan
American College, Rome

Mount St. Mary's College at Emmittsburg, Maryland, entering in the autumn of 1855 and remaining until the summer of 1857.

A glance at the portrait of young Corrigan—the open, bright eye, the pleasing smile, the full, well-rounded brow, the firmly framed reposeful face—assures one that the testimony of schoolmates and school records may be trusted. Good-humored, sensitive, enjoying all the sports of youth, modest, refined, studious, talented, and pious—such was the Michael Augustine Corrigan of St. Mary's and of Mount St. Mary's. In 1855-56, and again in 1856-57, his record was exceptional, taking, as he did, the class prize in Greek, Latin, mathematics, history, and French.

Thomas Corrigan had prospered with the years. Putting aside his trade, he ventured into business as a grocer; proved to be a wise manager; invested with foresight in Newark property; and in 1857, when fortunes were small, might be considered a well-to-do man. To Catherine, the oldest child and only daughter, a change of climate had been recommended, her health being delicate. Her favorite brother, Michael Augustine, seven years her junior, was chosen as her companion. Sailing from New York in the *North Star,* on September 5, they journeyed from Southampton to Havre, Paris, Dijon, Lyons, Marseilles, Genoa, Pisa, Leghorn, Civita Vecchia, Naples, and thence to Palermo. The famous city they entered on October 24.

After a stay of a couple of months in the Sicilian capital, they returned to Naples. In Rome, thanks to good letters, brother and sister found friends—friends they retained as long as life lasted. From Rome they travelled to Terni, Spoleto, Assisi, Perugia, Arezzo, Florence, Milan, Como, and finally to

Paris once more. There Catherine remained. On June 29, 1858, her brother sailed, in the *Fulton*, for home.

Were the school-fellows all dead, the college records destroyed, the ambrotype dimmed, faded, we should still find it easy to make a lifelike sketch of Michael Augustine at the age of eighteen; for in a diary of this journey, and in letters to his parents and brothers, he sketched himself unconsciously.

Thanks to the training of Bernard Kearney, no doubt, as well as to that of the two St. Mary's, he wrote English freely, correctly, and with a rare good taste. Of persons as well as things he was a keen observer. Nature he loved; art he admired judiciously. Imagination he had, fresh, lively. Details, historical or legendary, he accumulated rapidly; a sure memory retained them all. Journeying after the good old fashion, in *vettura* or *diligence,* he could associate with townspeople and villagers, and, after a leisurely fashion, inspect the natural beauties that crowd one another along the road he followed. Tact he possessed in a remarkable degree, and a prudence uncommon at his age. With a genial good humor he was full to overflowing—joyous. Though bashful, he was fond of companionship, and made agreeable acquaintances in all places. His faith was firm, soulful, lively; and his piety, like that of his sister, ardent. To brother and sister, the real world, the most beautiful world, was that one made up of the tombs of Christian martyrs, confessors, virgins; of altars grand or mean —altars of perpetual sacrifice; of grottoes, fountains, valleys, hilltops, reminiscent of the glories, the sorrows, the joys, the mercies of the Immaculate Mother. Pilgrimage after pilgrimage they made in Sicily, in Italy, in France.

With autumn, Michael Augustine returned to Emmittsburg. Graduating with the degree of A.B. in the summer of 1859, he gave new proofs of talent and of love for study. Not only did he carry off the class honors and a medal, but he also read a prize essay, whose subject was " The Uses of Beauty"—an essay showing, besides that rhetorical art of expression which so becomes the graduate, a pleasing culture acquired during his year of wandering.

Whatever had been his natural inclination, it was only now that, assured of a vocation, he told his parents of his intention to aspire to the priesthood. Bishop Bayley, to whom he and his family were well and most favorably known, forwarded the youth's plans; and provision was made for his entrance into the American College, which the hierarchy of the United States, in union with Pius IX, purposed opening at Rome in the fall of the same year.

Sailing in September, unaccompanied, he made a tour of Ireland, visiting affectionately the birthplace of his beloved father and mother, gathering, as his letters testify, a large knowledge of men; noting social, political, and religious conditions; singing with his gaily hospitable hosts, and, as before, laughing with the humorous and gently helping on their humor. " I laugh all the way," he writes " (there's so much to amuse by the wayside)—till I think of home—a sudden fit comes over me—and never am I as lonesome as then." From Dublin his route led him to London, and thence to Paris, where, as he notes, he visited his schoolmate at Wilmington, Mr. Henry A. Brann, then a seminarian at St. Sulpice, and with him passed a day at Versailles. By the same road his sister and himself had travelled in 1857, he went to Marseilles, and thence the same little steam " tub " carried him once more to Civita Vecchia. On the twenty-sixth of October he arrived in Rome; the morning following he reported to Mgr. Bedini, at Albano—the same Mgr. Bedini who had a few years before been welcomed so civilly in New York City by the polished gentlemen who then claimed to be the representatives of American ideas as they should be.

Noblesse oblige. Mgr. Bedini was the gracious patron of the American College. The old convent that, during nine years, had served as a barrack for the French soldiery became habitable under his supervision. Chapel and church he renovated and beautified; the lemon trees in the court were witnesses to his taste and care; the statue of the Immaculate Mother of God was lifted on high in his presence; and there, before Mary most blest, he was the first one to kneel, reciting the Rosary. If Mgr. Bedini owed a debt to America, he repaid it at Rome, in the Via Umiltà.

As the first student coming from the United States especially to seek admission to the American College, Michael Augustine Corrigan received a warm welcome. The " first fruits," Mgr. Bedini entitled him. The new college was unfinished, so that he, and those who soon followed him, were housed in the Urban College, familiarly known as " Propaganda." On the octave of All Saints, with his American companions, he first put on an ecclesiastical habit—that worn by the Propaganda students, the costume of the American College being as yet undetermined. Ceremoniously the college was opened on December 8, the feast of the Immaculate Conception—the patronal feast of the United States, Mgr. Bedini officiating. During the afternoon of the same day, a rector was chosen for the college: Father William McCloskey, the present venerable and venerated Bishop of Louisville. " Elegant scholarship, unfeigned humility, winning manners, and exquisite tact are all united in him "—thus, when he heard of the appointment, the future

Archbishop of New York, on November 17, 1859, in a letter to his sister Catherine, pictured the rector elect.

While awaiting the opening of the American College, neither he nor his fellow-students had been idle. Under the rules of the Urban College, they began their work. The course of philosophy Mr. Corrigan determined to enter. At Emmittsburg he had made a year's study of the great science, but now he looked upon the course there pursued as " fragmentary." Besides, he had acquired no habit of speaking Latin. Putting away, for a time, mathematics and Greek, he could compress the two years' philosophy into one. With freedom in the use of the Latin language, and with a thorough course of philosophy—thus he argued, and wisely argued—he would be the better prepared for " the proper understanding of theology."

The Rev. Dr. Bernard Smith, better known perhaps as Dom Bernardo or Abbot Smith, acted as rector of the American College until March, 1860, when Rector McCloskey arrived in Rome. Four years of seminary life passed under his prudently liberal rule brought many joys to Michael Augustine Corrigan; joys not unmixed with sorrow. Bright as his eyes were, they had never been strong. The Roman heat and glare tried them exceedingly, but, wearing green spectacles, he counted his eyes as useful as the best. A faithful, an anxious student, he has but one regret—the hours of study are too few. Visiting, according to the custom of the students, the monuments of Pagan and of Christian Rome, he familiarized himself with their history, legends, mechanical construction, architectural and artistic features; and this he did with sincerity, without vanity, with a keen power of observation; and, what is more characteristic, with delight, as his letters prove. During vacations, long or short; rambling; or when pilgriming to an old or a

new shrine of Our Lady, his pen is busy describing the pic-
turesque in nature, the human in men and women, the incidents
of a day or a week—incidents affecting, amusing, devotional,
instructive. The lives of the saints he has by heart; a church,
a convent, monastery, a ruin, recalls one, recalls another. He
tells their story. Neither preacher nor pedagogue, he is an
agreeable cicerone. " Rome grows on me more and more," he
writes in 1862, " but pagan admiration dies away and Christian
veneration grows stronger." Italy was in a turmoil, and so
was his own country. Hearing less of the latter than of the
former, he was all the more concerned. Of many interesting
facts illustrating the conditions in the Papal Rome of his day,
and, as well, the Franco-Sardinian-Garibaldian tragicomedy,
he has preserved the memory—facts that will bear the retelling.

Contented, nay, happy, he would have all others equally so.
To father, mother, sister, to grandmother, to brothers older
and younger, he is ever counselling cheerfulness: " cheerfulness is the secret of happiness: in trials let our endurance be
joyous." In corresponding with his family he is most dutiful, most affectionate. The youngest brother is remembered
equally with the venerable grandmother. To each one he writes
intimately, lovingly; and of every letter the substance and the
style, adapted with uncommon wisdom to the age, character,
pursuits, and, we may say, needs of the person addressed, evidence a mind accustomed to reflection and a generous heart.

Among the joys of seminary life, the most delectable to
him were those he experienced as, step by step, he was permitted to ascend higher and higher in the sanctuary: joys that
were complete when he stood in the priest's exalted station at
the altar of the Holy of Holies. Having received minor orders
a few days earlier, he was ordained subdeacon on March 21,

1863, in the Church of St. John Lateran. To the order of dea-
conship he was promoted in the same year, on the thirtieth of
August, the feast of St. Rose of Lima, Mgr. Pietro Villanova
Castellacci being the officiating prelate, and the place the private chapel of the Vicariate of Rome. By the hands of Cardinal
Patrizi, Vicar of Rome, on the nineteenth of September following,—the feast of St. Januarius and Companions, martyrs,—
in the same historic church in which the subdeaconship had
been conferred upon him, he was ordained a priest for the
diocese of Newark. On the following day, the feast of Our
Lady of the Seven Sorrows, in the church attached to the American College, on the altar dedicated to Our Lady of Guadalupe, in behalf of his beloved parents, he offered up his first
Mass. The choice of this altar, we venture to say, was a choice
inspired by gratitude; for, on the afternoon of December 8,
1859, before that altar, he, with his American fellow-students,
began a triduum in honor of this most condescending Lady.

Though not a singular favor, the advancement of Michael
Augustine Corrigan to the priesthood a year before the completion of his theological course was a favor and—may we not
say—a grace. At the end of his fourth year he purposed taking
the examination for the degree of Doctor of Divinity. Were
it not for the consolations of the priesthood, he might not have
borne with perfect resignation the trials a twelvemonth brought
him. With a deep wound in his heart, he presented himself
for examination toward the end of June, 1864, and won the
degree with honor.

Even a slight sketch of the life of Archbishop Corrigan
one should not attempt without narrating here—if one may be
pardoned the word—a romance; a spiritual romance, in which
he was one of the leading characters; a romance whose begin-

ning and ending doubtless influenced strongly his whole life. Perhaps when he set sail for Palermo, in September, 1857, with his sister Catherine, he knew that for nine years—ever since her sixteenth year—she had longed for a religious life. She was nineteen when, in 1851, she graduated at the Convent of the Sacred Heart, Manhattanville, New York, gaining the prize of "Excellence," a prize conferred on no other pupil until nigh fifty years afterward. Her father and mother were not unaware of her desire; but, blinded by fond affection for their oldest child and only daughter, they discouraged, if they did not wholly discountenance, a sentiment which was indeed a passion. In the winter of 1858, while brother and sister were in Rome, she disclosed her heart to him. There she would enter a convent. To live solely for God, in retirement, she felt an irresistible calling. He argued, protested again and again, but all in vain. As he wrote soon after: when he had ended, she stated her case, and then he was quickly vanquished. Nevertheless, she left Rome with him, travelling by the route we have recorded. In Paris she promptly sought the Convent of the Sacred Heart, and soon announced to him her decision to enter the novitiate at Conflans. His words were of no avail. She had counted the cost; so she thought. Her parents would freely acquiesce, convinced, as they must be, of the deliberation and conscientiousness of her act. The pain of parting would be spared them and herself. Besides, her novitiate over, she could return to her own country, and, as a nun, be near her family. A touching letter written by the brother to their mother, after his sister had forsaken him, displayed prudence, self-control, and tenderness. He condemns, defends, consoles, pleads, with that art which is natural only to a man religious, dutiful, gentle, sympathetic.

But the mother would not be consoled. Reason could not medicine to her sore heart. Such a parting she would not have. Her very life seemed to depend on the speedy return of Catherine. Bishop Bayley was appealed to; her oldest brother took the first steamer for France. At Conflans he presented a letter from the Bishop of Newark. Obediently the daughter returned home. Once more she devoted herself to comforting the aged grandmother, lightening a mother's cares, rejoicing a father; and, above all, to guiding and guarding her three youngest brothers, as she had guarded and guided Michael Augustine. Her mother had imagined she could bear a home parting; but once the only daughter was enfolded in her arms, she would ·hold her forever. The convent door, so it seemed, was barred.

However patiently borne, Catherine's burden was not light. Having tasted the sweets of the cloister, she coveted them daily. From the wise and faithful and gentle brother in Rome she received her chiefest support in her trial. He was entirely grateful to her, because, as he acknowledged, she was the one who, from boyhood, had kept him in the path of the seminary; gratitude was mingled with admiration, for now she had led a younger brother, James, to follow him to Rome. "A guardian angel " in their home he likens her to. Resigned as she tried to be, in the world as if she were of the world, there came moments of depression. Her health failed; failed more than mother or father dared to see. In October, 1863, she was permitted to accompany her brother James on his way to the American College. The winter in Italy would remove a lingering cold.

Rome, from which she parted so unwillingly in 1858, she reëntered on November 26, 1863. Nigh to the Pincian Hill she took an apartment, where her two brothers might conveniently visit her. For a time health promised a return; then, by degrees, the cough came more frequently, and pain made a companion of her. And now there were days when the effort of rising taxed her, and the bed was not irksome. A maid cared for her. Providence sent kind friends to the stranger—noble friends; friends attracted by the story of her extraordinary piety. Her room was a veritable oratory, where she passed the waking and wakeful hours of day and night in prayer, meditation, thanksgiving; in contrite expiation. So edified was her spiritual director, that he not only permitted, but counselled, her to make a private vow—a vow which was put in writing and was signed by her.

Spring came—an unkindly spring that drove even hope away. The physician advised Catherine to leave the Holy City. Starting at once, she could, he imagined, reach home alive. The thought that, before dying, she would see mother and father, and that she might enkindle in their hearts a still more generous love of God, cheered her. But who would accompany her? A good French religious, a trained nurse, a sister of the Hospitallers of St. Augustine, in Rome temporarily, hearing of the exemplary American woman who was ill, visited her charitably. Learning the circumstances, she offered to accompany the patient to France, and to care for her until she sailed for home. On the twenty-second of May Catherine bade farewell to her brothers. At Marseilles and again at Paris she rested; the journey taxed her enfeebled body. From Paris, on the first of June, she was conveyed to Meaux,—Bossuet's Meaux,—where the Augustinian sisters had a convent. There she took to her bed, realizing at last that her earthly home she would never see with human eyes.

Suffering much, she suffered most patiently; winning not

only affection but also reverence from the good religious around her. Ever most devout to the Blessed Virgin Mary, she was now more lovingly so. With the Sacred Heart of Our Lord she communed intimately. She asked to be allowed to make her profession as an Augustinian sister. The granting of such a request, to one who had not been even a novice, would be uncommon. To the Bishop of Meaux, as of right, the question was referred. Not merely consenting, he brought to herself the news of his consent. Her rare virtues were known to him.

An altar was set up in her room, before it her religious habit was blessed; she received it from the celebrant. Her brow was crowned with a wreath of white roses as she wept in a transport of joy. Veiled, the roses gave way to a crown of thorns; her hair had been shorn. With a crucifix on her breast, a lighted taper in her hand, having spoken her vows firmly, all the members of her new family listening, she signed them with her own hand. Amélie—beloved of God—is the name they gave her.

Early on the morning of the feast of the Purification of the Blessed Virgin, still wearing the bridal veil, the crucifix still on her breast, the crown of thorns on her forehead, she received, in the presence of the community, the Viaticum. Soon afterward she asked for the sacrament of Extreme Unction. Her wish was fulfilled. At midday of the beautiful feast, the mind being perfectly conscious, her hallowed soul forsook her chaste and chastened body. Clothed in the Augustinian habit, her bier surrounded with white flowers, her spiritual sisters, more numerous than her brothers in the flesh, all in choir dress, bearing lighted candles, bore her remains to the convent cemetery.

" Convinced of her perfect happiness," wrote the charitable sister—one is tempted to mention the name—who nursed her on the way from Rome to Meaux, " I sang a ' Magnificat,' in thanksgiving, as soon as I had word of her death. 'Blessed' I called her."

And her beloved brother? He saw her grave, not herself; a grave that he revisited on July 7, 1900, as he returned from his last journey to Rome. Inside of the laurel crown of the Doctor of Divinity there were sharp thorns, whose wounds he could not disclose. What were they compared with those of a stricken mother and father! To his quick perception, apt choice of means to an end, delicacy, tenderness of heart, we have already paid a tribute based on sure knowledge. Now he exceeds himself. To each parent his letters brought something more than a spirit of Christian resignation to the will of God; something more than human comfort. They brought a deep feeling of gratitude to a loving Providence—gratitude for a visible, indeed a marvellous blessing. To-day the grave of Sister Amélie is held in veneration at Meaux. Should one be charged with imprudence, saying that, dead, the influence of this unselfish, blessed sister on Michael Augustine Corrigan's after life was no less real, effective, beneficial—he cherished her sweet memory lovingly to the end, wearing about his neck her medal of the Blessed Virgin Mary and the signed vow she made in Rome—than her living influence had been on his boyhood, youth, and early manhood!

Arriving in Newark on September 5, 1864, Dr. Corrigan, placing first the higher duty, reported forthwith to his bishop, and then sought his happy, grieving parents. Appointed to succeed his former fellow-student in Wilmington and in Rome, Rev. Henry A. Brann, D.D., he assumed the professorship

The Reverend M. A. Corrigan, D.D.
President of Seton Hall College
1868

of dogmatic theology and of Sacred Scripture at the Seton Hall Seminary of the Immaculate Conception, South Orange, New Jersey. Though promoted in 1865 to the vice-presidency of Seton Hall College, and also to the directorship of the Seminary, at the solicitation of the reverend president, Bernard J. McQuaid—who, reserving due credit to the distinguished Bishop Bayley, might well be called the founder of both college and seminary—Dr. Corrigan confined his labors especially to the seminary until the deserved appointment, in July, 1868, of President McQuaid to the newly established episcopal see of Rochester, New York. The offices so long and so honorably held by Father McQuaid in college and seminary were now conferred on Dr. Corrigan; and in October, 1868, still retaining these offices, he was named by Bishop Bayley as vicar-general of the diocese of Newark, a position that Father McQuaid also had occupied. Twice during the succeeding four years Dr. Corrigan acted as administrator of the diocese: first when, in 1870, at the opening of the Vatican Council, Bishop Bayley was called to Rome by Pius IX; and a second time when the same prelate received the nomination to the archiepiscopal see of Baltimore.

Besides dogmatic theology and Sacred Scripture, Dr. Corrigan, during these eight years, taught in the seminary moral theology, liturgy, and church history; lecturing also in Seton Hall College on profane history and on the evidences of the Christian religion; and, for a time, giving lessons in Latin to scholars far advanced. The appointment, in 1868,— the year following his return from Rome and his ordination at Seton Hall,—of his brother, Rev. James H. Corrigan, as director of the seminary, lightened in a measure the responsibilities of Dr. Corrigan, without diminishing his labors.

A tireless student, he took no recreation other than that accorded to the seminarians. Indeed, all the rules by which they were bound he obeyed freely. Favorites he had none, either in or out of class. Deeply respected by them, he treated his pupils rather as if he were only a senior student, and not a superior. As a teacher he was patient and thorough. In his lectures he seemed to exhaust a subject. Until his appointment to the presidency of Seton Hall College he had no association with the pupils of that institution, but afterward his relations with them were not merely friendly, they were affectionate. Just, he was almost brotherly in dealing with them.

To Seton Hall Dr. Corrigan had been more than a president; with two of his brothers, Rev. James H. and Joseph F. Corrigan, M.D., he had been its preserver. Timid about its financial prospects, Bishop Bayley was on the point of transferring it to a religious order, when the three brothers offered, and in fact bound themselves in writing, to provide a considerable capital, should the same be needed, in order to assure that the diocese should be freed from all risk of an extraordinary tax for its support. Under the youthful president's administration, the courses of study were ordered anew and methods were revised. The college buildings and grounds were materially improved; and the chapel, enlarged and adorned, was dedicated. The institution prospered. On the Board of Trustees ecclesiastics and laymen of eminence were pleased to serve. Former benefactors and patrons remained true; new friends among the clergy and laity were attracted by the learning, ability, and intelligent zeal of Dr. Corrigan. A burse, bearing the family name, two of his brothers, Philip and Joseph F. Corrigan, M.D., founded.

Few men have been better equipped for the exacting office of a bishop than Dr. Corrigan was when, in February, 1873, he received word of his elevation to the see of Newark—an honor unsought, and that he would gladly have forgone. Added griefs, one and another and another, had strained his heart-strings. In July, 1865, at the age of eighty-three, the venerated grandmother died; a handsome woman, of a dignified bearing, a strong, vivacious character, to whom he was attached by an affectionate sentiment not second to her own. Within less than two years, on January 5, 1867, his revered father had been carried off without a moment's warning. The loved, the loving mother, Catherine's mother, he and his brothers laid in the grave on August 31, 1869. How humbly and proudly father and mother would have kneeled at his feet to receive a heartfelt episcopal benediction—the blessing of gratitude! Inasmuch as nature disposes a man, he owed certain characteristics to father and to mother; she, like her own mother, being of a nervous temperament, energetic, and rarely well endowed mentally; while the father was gentle in manner, slow of speech, charitable in word and deed; in all things moderate and modest; a man of good practical sense and most industrious.

Consecrated on May 4, 1873, in St. Patrick's Cathedral, Newark, by His Grace Archbishop McCloskey of New York, Michael Augustine Corrigan was welcomed not only by the bishops of the province, by the priests of the diocese, and by the laity, but also by many non-Catholics who had learned to esteem his virtues and his courtesy. To the clergy he was no stranger; the younger men had been guided by him in the seminary; as vicar-general or as administrator of the diocese, all had been subject to his rule.

Seton Hall he made his official residence, though his duties more frequently compelled him to pass three days of each week in the parish house of the cathedral, whose rector, Mgr. George H. Doane, succeeding Father Bernard J. McQuaid, became, in time, the vicar-general of the new bishop.

Seven years of unceasing activity, prudent enterprise, patience, courage, and always of gentleness, of charity—thus, in few words, one may sum up the episcopal rule of Bishop Corrigan in the diocese of Newark—a diocese which, divided only after his promotion to a higher post of duty, comprised in his day the whole State of New Jersey. Entering office, he was confronted by a serious financial problem in a conspicuous parish—a problem not of his making, and one that would have tested the executive ability of men even more experienced. With the hearty, generous support of clergy and laity, and at a cost to his patrimony of ten thousand dollars, the problem was in good time and happily solved; the credit of the Catholics of the whole diocese being, at the same time, permanently and solidly established.

The waifs of the diocese appealed to him; the neglected boys and girls whose health, morals, souls were endangered. A protectory soon housed and cared for the one sex; in a House of the Good Shepherd the girls too were guarded and trained. To the orphans he was a devoted father. Close by St. Patrick's rectory stood the asylum. Hardly a day passed there, when he was in the city, without a visit from the bishop— just to watch over the children, to say pleasant words' to them, to lighten their hearts, and to encourage the motherly Sisters of Charity. In the hospitals he could be found when a Confirmation or any needed sacrament was urgent. A sick-call he answered gladly; and there were times when, being the

The Right Reverend Michael Augustine Corrigan, D.D.

Bishop of Newark

1874

only ecclesiastic who spoke Italian, he hastened out of the city to comfort a dying immigrant. Returning from Europe in August, 1877, fatally ill, Bishop Bayley sought rest amid the scenes of his first episcopal labors, and in the company of friends to whom he had long been attached. There, on the third of the following October, twenty-four years after his consecration to the see of Newark, in St. Patrick's rectory, he found rest, an eternal rest. At the hands of Michael Augustine Corrigan he must have known that he would receive an attention sincerely filial—an attention he deserved—and such an attention he did receive. Suffering intensely, the Archbishop constantly craved the comfort of the Bishop's presence in the sick-room. To read to the patient, piously or lightly, to distract pleasingly, to assist, became a part of the daily routine of duty—of a grateful, sympathetic service that, ending late at night, began again long before daybreak.

During Bishop Corrigan's administration the number of parish and mission churches in the diocese increased from one hundred and twenty-one to one hundred and eighty-two; the number of parochial schools was doubled, and more than doubled; new orphanages, new asylums, new academies were instituted. In Jersey City a college was opened by the learned Jesuit fathers. Communities of religious women, vowed to a life of charitable work, the Bishop fostered. His cathedral—the ground for which had been purchased nigh thirty years earlier by his faithful friend, Father Moran, the pastor of old St. John's during his boyhood—freed at last from debt, he consecrated in 1876.

Only in this year did Bishop Corrigan resign the presidency of Seton Hall College, a resignation that implied no severance of the intimate relations of the past twelve years. As a mem-

ber of the board of trustees—an office held by him until 1891—
and as bishop, he continued to show a lively interest in the
progress of the institute to which he was bound by the many
ties formed both as a teacher and as a governor. Knowing well
the tradition of the Church, his watchful eye was ever directed to the seminary, the garden in which the very seed
of the Church is planted and cultured. Choosing competent
and earnest professors, and broadening the courses of study,
his aim was not simply to send forth priests intellectual in their
tastes, but it was especially to train men who, fixed in the ways
of virtue and decorous in manner, would be calm and zealous
in the performance of all the priestly duties. In order that,
once out of the seminary, and burdened by the cares of the
ministry, the clergy should not be satisfied with the sole pur-
suit of literary or of scientific studies, or perhaps distracted
by vainer gratifications, he, following a wise rule of the Church
—one constantly lauded by the Roman pontiffs, though one
hitherto unpractised in the diocese—assembled the clergy,
quarterly, for the explication in writing and in speech, and for
the discussion, of theological questions, doctrinal and moral,
and, as well, of questions of ritual.

Subject in part to New York and in part to Philadelphia
until 1853, it was only by slow degrees that, among the small
and scattered Catholic communities of New Jersey, served
originally by priests who, because of the necessities of the
times, could have no tenure whatsoever as parish rectors, certain abuses of law in the administration of the sacraments
could be corrected. An instance of one of these abuses the
Bishop had before him in his own case; the sacrament of
Baptism having been conferred on him, according to the custom of the day, in the house of his parents. How uncere-

monious the celebration of the sacred offices of the Church had
been, and continued to be, may be estimated from the experience of Father Moran, who, though he had been almost
thirty years a priest of the diocese, yet for the first time offi-
ciated at a solemn Mass during the obsequies of Eleanor
Hoey English in 1865. Twice, in 1856 and in 1868, looking
to the due ordering of priests and people through the inculca-
tion of a more exact knowledge of the law and through a closer
application of its requirements, Bishop Bayley had united the
clergy in a diocesan synod. Only in 1878, after having by
studious and reflective observation made, himself thoroughly
acquainted with the conditions prevailing in his rapidly growing charge, did Bishop Corrigan call the third Newark Synod—
a synod that was considerately followed by a fourth, in the very
next year.

Should there be any one who doubts the learning of the
Bishop, the clearness, the precision, the logical power of his
mind, the ease, sincerity, and moderation of his manner of expression—an ease not hampered by the Latin language—the
modesty of the man, and his loving reverence for the holy
office of the priesthood of Jesus Christ, the doubter may ser-
viceably consult the little volume in which the statutes promulgated in the Third Synod are preserved, comparing
them with those handed down to him by his distinguished predecessor. Taking no credit to himself, Bishop Corrigan not
only revised, reordered, reinforced the standing local laws, but
he also amended, developed, clarified them; adding, besides,
such regulations as were of obligation in order to conform with
the decrees of the Second Plenary Council of Baltimore, and
with the latest decisions of the sacred congregations. By refer-
ence to authorities, the statutes were fortified, as well as by a

lucid presentation of the doctrine or custom of the Church on all the subjects involved.

A resemblance between Michael Augustine Corrigan and St. Francis of Assisi has been suggested by a writer in the press and by an illustrious archbishop. Certainly, inasmuch as we measure the one with the other by their veneration for the temple of the Divine Majesty, for all Christ's sacraments, and above all for the "Mystery of Faith"; by their zeal for the decency of divine worship, and their conscientious, enlightened, and, consequently, punctilious care that obedience to the very letter of the sacred liturgy should be perfect, these two were one in heart and soul. Influenced—nay, rather, compelled—by these motives, the Bishop of Newark at an early day advised his clergy of an intention to make, systematically, the episcopal visitations required by the Canons. And these visitations he thereafter performed at regular intervals, and most thoroughly, observing acutely every detail. The conditions he found in each church were by him set down in writing. According to these records—records that are at hand—pastors were commended or corrected.

Because of the Bishop's patiently acquired habit of method, it would cost only the time used in copying to detail here every public act of his industrious life in Newark: pastorals, ordinations, the laying of corner-stones, receptions of religious, dedication of churches, confirmations, retreats, marriages, meetings of diocesan committees, letters open or quasi-private, speeches in Latin or English, instructions and sermons. Of all the priests of the diocese, secular and regular, he personally compiled a list, with the dates of appointment, change of place, absence or death. The progress of the ecclesiastical students he recorded with equal care: where and what they were studying, their rank in class, and their date of ordination. Warned by his early experience, he had taken simple measures to control the finances of every parish in the diocese. Through the annual reports he first exacted from the pastors, at a glance he could tell the income and the debt of each church subject to him. Receiving all reports and comparing, he exercised a proper control over the finances of the diocese as a whole, and over each part. The annual baptisms and marriages, church by church, he also made a note of,—doing all this work with his own hand. At any minute he could take a view, general or particular, of his charge. Theologian, legist, rubricist, he was also an archivist. So well was this recognized, that Archbishop Bayley, entering the see of Baltimore, sent for Dr. Corrigan to put in order and to systematize the records of that comparatively ancient see.

One important item we have not forgotten, but indeed most deliberately reserved—an item concerning parochial schools. By speech, sermon, writing, by public acts, from the day of his consecration, and thereafter by a renewal of the diocesan statute, Bishop Corrigan warned, urged, encouraged, commanded clergy and laity to build, patronize, support, improve the parochial school, as a protection to faith, to morals, and as a guarantee of the healthful prosperity of the citizen. How earnest he was, how wisely insistent—and the value men set upon a right principle, intelligently stated and firmly pressed—one may gather from the record. When, in 1880, he left the diocese, in every parish except thirty-two a parochial school had been established; and the parishes lacking schools were so small and so poor as to be patently excusable.

The promotion of Bishop Corrigan to New York as the coadjutor of Cardinal McCloskey, however unexpected by the laity, was not a complete surprise to either prelate. For several years, because of declining health and increasing labor, the Cardinal had been considering the choice of an auxiliary or of a coadjutor. Finally, in the spring of 1880 he consulted his suffragans. His choice they made their own. Of the three names selected for presentation to Rome, Bishop Corrigan's was one. For the removal of his name from the list he pleaded strongly. Unanimously, Cardinal and fellow-suffragans insisted. Only after the lapse of several months did he learn that, meantime, the Cardinal had advised the Holy See of his preference for the Bishop of Newark. Writing at once to the Prefect of Propaganda, Cardinal Simeoni, the Bishop begged that his name be withdrawn. The answer was that, if appointed by the Pope, his duty was obedience. On the twenty-seventh of September he had word of his nomination. Late in October came the papal bulls appointing him Archbishop of Petra and coadjutor to the Archbishop of New York, with the right of succession. It is worthy of note that when, in August, 1863, Mr. Corrigan was ordained a subdeacon, the celebrant, Mgr. Castellacci, was the titular of the see of Petra; a title later held by Mgr. Ruffo Scilla and also by the present illustrious Prefect of Propaganda, His Eminence Cardinal Girolamo Maria Gotti.

Congratulated on all sides, publicly honored, praised by his diocesan clergy, his seminarians, the college students, the religious under his charge, the laity, old and young; by many non-Catholics, and by the greater number of the prelates of the country; welcomed publicly in New York—the young Archbishop of Petra—but forty-one years of age—making his home in the seat of the archdiocese on the octave of All Saints, 1880, entered upon his new office, not as one whose ambition had been gratified, but as one upon whose shoulders a heavy cross had been laid. " No doubt," thus he wrote four days after hearing of the appointment, " the cross is much heavier than I have any adequate conception of; and its weight will only be fully known with time." And immediately he consoles himself with the reflection that " one's graces are found in doing the will of God, not one's own will."

Full five years Archbishop Corrigan occupied the post of coadjutor. No administrative power did he exercise during this period of time; he had no such power, except as the same might be momentarily conferred upon him by Cardinal Mc-Closkey, who, up to the date of his death, governed through his vicars-general, Mgr. Quinn and Mgr. Preston. Only with October 10, 1885, did the rule of Archbishop Corrigan over the archdiocese of New York actually begin.

Providence had so disposed that, before his elevation to the see of Newark, Dr. Corrigan enjoyed the advantage of a rare training as a professor, as director of a seminary, as a college president, as a vicar-general, as a diocesan administrator; not to speak of the training he had been careful to acquire as a confessor and preacher at Seton Hall and at the neighboring mission church, which he served voluntarily. To his training in these offices had been added the seven years of episcopal government. Now, in New York, he was to have five years of especial training, under the eyes of a cool-minded, most experienced, polished, sincere, and devout superior; five years to observe, to know—well advised—both clergy and laity; to learn the traditions and methods of the see; to measure the needs of the people; to outline a policy. Nay, more, he was to have the benefit of five years of study. A student, not merely because he loved learning, but also because he regarded learning as a conscientious duty, Bishop Corrigan, though the hours had been compulsorily shortened, continued while in the Newark diocese to be a daily student, just as Mr. Corrigan, Father Corrigan, Dr. Corrigan, had been. More than ever a student was the Archbishop of Petra; and, at the end of the five years, more than ever a scholar.

The powers exercised by the Archbishop of Petra were, therefore, principally those of order: the consecration or dedication of churches, ordaining of priests, administration of other sacraments, laying of corner-stones, pontificating on solemn feasts. Lesser duties were also committed to him: attending college and convent commencements, preaching at church celebrations, speaking at public or private functions. Important duties, too, he fulfilled, such as the carrying on of official correspondence demanding more than ordinary privacy or care. In the early days, until the see of Newark had been filled, he served his first diocese as if he were still a part of it. And a part of it he was. To leave his native city, the old home of his parents; to be separated from his brothers; from the clergy he affectionately trained; from the college and the seminary where he had passed so many happy years; from the schools, convents, hospitals, charitable institutions of all sorts that he had lovingly created and as lovingly nurtured; to sever the ties that bound him to sincere friends; friends of youth, friends of the riper years— all this cost him naturally more than one regret; regret that time may not have lessened. The meaning of the word "turmoil" he knew partly; what was in store for him he could fortunately not foresee.

Upon the death of the beloved Cardinal McCloskey, to whose conservative rule the archdiocese of New York owed so much, the Archbishop of Petra, on October 10, 1885, succeeded to the title and charge of Archbishop of New York; though the pallium was conferred upon him only on the fourth of March of the following year.

Bishop Corrigan's respect for law, familiarity with the law, appreciation of the benefit necessarily associated with the gradual operation of wisely developed legislation, he had proved. In the archdiocese of New York he was not permitted to wait until 1885 in order to apply his ecclesiastical erudition and his wisdom to public uses. The Cardinal and his suffragans knew the man. Purposing to assemble the bishops of the archdiocese in a provincial council, to the end that the existing general law should be affirmed, emendated, unified, adapted to the immediate future as well as to the present, the Cardinal charged his coadjutor with the duty of preparing a complete scheme of legislation for the province of New York. Called to Rome by His Holiness Leo XIII in the autumn of 1883, as were all the archbishops in the United States, to consult over the legislation to be submitted to the third plenary council of the Catholic Church in the United States of North America, a council held in Baltimore during the months of November and December, 1884, Cardinal McCloskey sent the Archbishop of Petra as his representative. A draft of the decrees collated by Archbishop Corrigan for the New York provincial council not only met with the approval of the Sacred Congregation of Propaganda, but then and there a goodly number of the decrees by him proposed were introduced into the legislative scheme adopted at Rome for the consideration of the Baltimore council. Their enactment by the American hierarchy at the plenary council explains the identity of many of the decrees printed in the official reports of the New York and of the Baltimore councils.

Again, as the representative of Cardinal McCloskey, the Archbishop of Petra attended the third plenary council at Baltimore, where, because of his acknowledged learning, his modestly expressed views were not without influence upon his fellow-prelates. Indeed, until his death, by members of the hierarchy he was often consulted on questions of doctrine, morals, canon law, rubrics, on forms of procedure, and on methods of administration, being expert in all—expert without pretension.

In the diocese of New York, prior to his accession, synods of the clergy were called at irregular intervals, the first having been held in 1842 and the fourth in 1883. On November 17, 1886, Archbishop Corrigan opened the fifth diocesan synod, and every third year thereafter he convoked the clergy to a synodal meeting. The text of the decrees promulgated in 1886, slightly amended from time to time so as to keep them in complete harmony with the most recent decrees of one or another of the Roman Congregations, holds to this day. Of this text one may repeat what has been already said of the order, precision, learning, apt expression, moderation, and piety that marked the matter and the manner of his first Newark synod.

To emphasize his reverent affection for the priesthood, his sense of the obligation of providing for its intellectual and moral standing and likewise for its comfort, the mention of the new seminary at Dunwoodie will suffice— a seminary that, materially at least, is not surpassed in Europe or on this continent. However, the Archbishop had not waited until 1891, when he announced the purchase of a site for the seminary, to show a true interest in his clergy. Under Cardinal McCloskey theological conferences had been introduced. Developing these, attending

The Most Reverend Michael Augustine Corrigan, D.D.

them all, showing his lively interest in them by reading every one of the written theses presented there, Archbishop Corrigan assured a closer application to the study of theology, an assurance made doubly sure in the case of the junior clergy by the examinations to which, during each of the five years immediately succeeding their ordination, they were and are subjected.

The rapid, the extraordinary growth of the archdiocese of New York had taxed even his able predecessors. To develop the system of government so that, with due facility, all the demands made upon it could be answered, a way had not yet been found. Archbishop Corrigan reorganized the system. There had been a diocesan council, honorary rather than active. To this council he gave a legal form, legal duties; the chancery system he remodelled, the finances of each church in the archdiocese he brought not only under the eyes of his vicars-general, but also under his own eyes. Irremovable rectors were designated. Rural deans were appointed to supervise local affairs; in time the parochial schools were placed under an ecclesiastical superintendent; for the city and for various subdivisions of the archdiocese school boards were named; a board of examiners was created—a board whose certificate was necessary in order to receive an appointment as a teacher in a parochial school; over all Catholic charities an ecclesiastical supervisor was appointed.

During the seventeen years of Archbishop Corrigan's rule the churches, chapels, and stations of the archdiocese were increased by one hundred and eighty-eight. To the number of the clergy two hundred and eighty-four were added; seventy-five new schools were opened. Not only were the existing charities fostered, but new demands, to the number of thirty and more, were supplied: day nurseries, hospitals, schools for the blind, for deaf mutes, industrial and reform schools, homes for immigrants. The labors of the Archbishop of New York were not limited to governing and overseeing. Besides the routine of episcopal duties, the ordinations, blessing of altars or of churches, consecrations, and the solemn offices of his cathedral, the tax of administering the sacrament of Confirmation was by itself a heavy one; from his coming in 1880 to the close of the year 1895—in which year the Right Rev. John M. Farley, D.D., becoming his auxiliary, divided the labors with him—he conferred this sacrament, to be exact, on one hundred and ninety-four thousand six hundred and seventy-eight persons. Even with the aid of a most efficient auxiliary, if we except the year 1900, when the Archbishop paid the visit *ad limina*, his share of this exacting duty was counted by thousands—from six to nine thousand annually.

As in Newark so in New York, the canonical visitation of all the churches of the diocese he made periodically and with vigilance. Of defects observed, pastors were promptly informed, in the Archbishop's own handwriting, as they were of oversights in the annual statements of parish accounts. President of the board of trustees of the cathedral, of the orphan asylum board, of the trustees of the seminary, of the Mission of the Immaculate Conception, of the trustees of the association for infirm priests of the diocese, of the council of the Sisters of Charity, he attended all meetings with regularity, advising everywhere modestly and wisely. Through his vicars-general, Mgr. Preston and Mgr. Donnelly, and their successors, Mgr. Farley and Mgr. Mooney, all the ordinary affairs of the diocese were administered. Every Friday morning he gave to his vicars-general.

Graciously he accepted from the rectors of churches, great

and small, invitations to pontificate at mass or at vespers or to preach on festal days; all the religious orders of men he favored in like ways. To jubilees or anniversaries of convents and academies, to receptions or professions of nuns or sisters, to the closing exercises of retreats, an invitation to the Archbishop was certain to bring a kindly acceptance. Struggling sisterhoods could command his presence whenever a kind word would encourage them or win friends to assist them. At college commencements every prizeman and graduate had a pleasing smile from him as he handed to one a diploma, to another a medal.

Among the charities of the archdiocese he showed an especial interest in the protectory, the foundling asylum, and the orphan asylum. Here, as in Newark, the orphans were most favored by him. From the episcopal house he made running visits, almost daily visits, to see them; no stranger guest parted from him without a greeting to and from the orphans. At the hospitals it was not merely to give sacraments that he called. Spare half hours he created in order to comfort the sick. Before he began to build the seminary impecunious sisterhoods, poor parishes, worthy charities could count on unasked donations from the Archbishop.

With his right reverend suffragans his official relations were most amicable. Esteeming his virtues, ability, zeal, they deferred to his learning, to his rightmindedness, as well as to his authority; and yet in their company he was but the first among equals. All those now happily ruling he had consecrated, if we except their dean, the venerable patron of his youth and the faithful friend during his life, Mgr. McQuaid, of the see of Rochester. To his priests the Archbishop was more than courteous. At any hour of the day, unless when work or an engagement absolutely hindered, he was at their service, and always with kind words even when correction was not un-earned. By the laity he was no less approachable. With them his office not unfrequently associated him as an arbiter among angry disputants, a peacemaker in families divided, a pro-tector of honor endangered if not lost, an adviser, a comforter in sore trials. His charity in all these cases made no measure of time, labor, of money if need be.

Every Catholic bishop has a bride—his cathedral—to which it is his duty to show an affectionate regard, enhancing comeli-ness by a chaste ornamentation, beautiful apparel; showing besides a solicitous desire for an honorable maintenance. The new spires of St. Patrick's, the chime of bells, the many aisle-chapels and the altars therein; the statues of Doctors of the Church, of Apostles, Evangelists, Confessors, Virgins; the sta-tions of the Cross, the rich vestments and sacred utensils—all these are lasting evidences of the fidelity of Archbishop Corri-gan to his church bride.

Besides the spacious seminary, he added to the diocesan buildings the two stately orphan asylums for boys and for girls, and the Boland School, in which he was about to inaugu-rate a preparatory seminary. With what delight did he wit-ness on July 20, 1901, the removal of the first spadeful of earth from the site of the new Cathedral Lady-chapel—a precious ex-ample of private munificence—to whose plan and architectural detail he had devoted so much thought and attention! The publicly known benefactions of Archbishop Corrigan were most generous. To Seton Hall College in June, 1884, he con-tributed nine thousand dollars as a fund for a burse; the beau-tiful chapel of St. Joseph's Seminary at Dunwoodie, begun and completed at his sole expense, the cost being sixty thousand

The Lady Chapel (Kelly Memorial), St. Patrick's Cathedral, New York

dollars, not only absorbed the greater part of his patrimony, but also every dollar that came to him from lay friends; to the library of the seminary, besides many valuable volumes, he donated the sum of ten thousand dollars; the altar of St. John the Evangelist in his cathedral, set up in memory of his predecessors in the see of New York,—John Connolly, O.P., John Dubois, John Hughes, and Cardinal John McCloskey,—was the gift of Michael Augustine Corrigan. Privately he advanced considerable sums to charitable institutions and to lay folk in straits—advances that often grew to be gifts, because of his gracious way of discharging the debts of others to himself. Calls made upon him by the deserving for aid in finding employment commanded anxious and untiring service. Known as he was the world over, letters came to him from strangers in many lands who were seeking stray relations. To these he gave the most faithful attention, however slight the indications, persisting as long as persistence admitted hope. Never did he dismiss unattended a letter of this character.

Outside of the archdiocese the meetings of the archbishops of the United States summoned him; and so did his duties as secretary and treasurer of the executive board of the Catholic University of Washington, duties he fulfilled as conscientiously as he did all others. In fact, only his deep sense of duty could have prompted his attendance at a meeting of the University board a few weeks before his lamented death, when the precarious condition of his health should have held him at home.

It was Mr. Elihu Root, the present secretary of war, who, in a speech delivered on May 1, 1898, at the public celebration of the twenty-fifth anniversary of Archbishop Corrigan's episcopate, said of him: ''He has been manly, dignified, and courteous in his social intercourse, contributing to the grace and charm of life." There was no compliment in these words; they expressed heartily the sentiments of all those that had ever enjoyed the pleasure of meeting the Archbishop socially. As a host or as a guest he was equally agreeable, attractive, whether among rich or poor, Catholics or non-Catholics. Always good-humored, ready to converse on the topics of the day, prompt with a timely anecdote, thoughtful of each one in the company, polished, modest, more interested in bringing out another's entertaining qualities than in displaying his own, unpretentious in dress as well as in manner, and seemingly unconscious of his distinction, he won sincere respect and cordial good will everywhere. The promise of his youth bore new fruit each year. "Charming" is the epithet applied to him by a distinguished prelate of the Newark diocese, one knowing him from his youth and for years living in the same house with him as bishop: "charming with all his priests and with all persons, the most pleasant of pleasant companions."

In 1880, immediately after hearing of his promotion to the see of New York, Bishop Corrigan ventured to forecast a heavy cross, one whose full weight should be known only with time. When time laid a heavy cross upon his shoulders he bore it bravely, patiently, and, as far as men saw, with the cheerfulness that in early youth he had rightly convinced himself to be the secret of happiness. Silent as he was during the harassing trials that beset him for years, he would have borne them even more silently were it not for the appeals of the laity, who deemed total silence on his part inopportune lest the episcopal authority might be weakened and grave injury be done to the cause of religion. Some persons represented the Archbishop then and thereafter as the maker of certain ecclesiastical policies in the United States, and the leader among the hierarchy in urging these policies. Time proved conclusively that he had been no more than he aimed to be—an archbishop who defended frankly and with courage the whole doctrine of the Catholic Church, who obeyed dutifully every decision of the Holy See, and who waited not in advising his flock of the warnings, instructions, judgments that issued from that Centre of Truth.

Of the reckless attacks made upon him, some, because of their malice, wounded him. Few men would have consoled themselves, as he did, with the thought that there must come a time when even malice would exhaust itself. Quietly, assiduously, he performed the duties of each day, devising meantime new measures by which the spiritual welfare of all those committed to his pastoral care might be advanced.

One malevolent insinuation he did not leave unnoticed—the insinuation that he had been false to his episcopal oath. With great dignity, by the admirable sermon he delivered on August 15, 1893, in St. Patrick's Cathedral, Mgr. Satolli, the Apostolic Delegate, being present, Archbishop Corrigan, while disdaining to answer those who had maligned him, still effectually closed their lips. Hardly had he entered upon the duties of a professor in Seton Hall when he began to inculcate publicly the necessity of Catholic unity with the see of Peter; of humble obedience to the teachings, monitions, decrees emanating from the Vicar of Christ. As bishop, as archbishop, from the pulpit, from the platform, in synods, in the retreats of the clergy, through letters to the clergy, through pastorals, he had reiterated the teachings of the earlier, priestly days. No one of his brethren preceded him in the publication of Papal briefs or encyclicals; even those addressed to nations other than our own were often noticed officially by him. The office conferred

upon Archbishop Corrigan by His Holiness the illustrious
Leo XIII on May 4, 1887,—the office of Prelate Assistant at
the Pontifical throne, a dignity reserved to noted Defenders of
the Faith,—testified to the estimation in which he was held at
Rome itself. Charitable, indeed, was he when his honor, his
faith, being assailed, he repeated in his cathedral pulpit the
prayer of his Divine Master, "Father, forgive them, for they
know not what they do."

Just as upon his installation the clergy and laity of New
York had welcomed Archbishop Corrigan, so during his firm
and benign rule they bore witness publicly again and again
to the affection, the devotion, the admiration that his holy life,
incessant labors, and fearless vindication of law, of order, of
right principle had compelled. Especially notable were the
manifestations of regard offered to him on September 20, 1888,
the twenty-fifth anniversary of his ordination to the priesthood,
and on May 4, 1898, when he celebrated the twenty-fifth anniversary of his consecration as bishop. Not alone from laymen
and priests and from eminent members of the hierarchy did
he receive on these memorable days outspoken tributes of
esteem, confidence, good will, but from many also who, though
not of his faith, had learned to appreciate justly his virtues
as an ecclesiastic and his liberality and patriotism as a citizen.
"Ever mindful of the public good," said Mr. Elbridge T.
Gerry at the reception tendered the Archbishop on the night
of May 4, 1898, "his efforts have resulted in the enlarging and
increasing of the prosperity of what is now known as the City
of New York." A " son of Puritan New England," Mr. Root,
at the same meeting, having described him as one who had been
"upright and just and kindly to all men," added these words:
" He has been a great conservative force, maintaining the
social order of civilization against all socialistic and anarchis-

tic attacks, maintaining the rights of property, on which our homes and the rewards of honest toil and the hopes of honorable ambition all depend.''

Nor were words of praise the only tokens of reverent friendship he received on the jubilee day of his episcopate. From the hands of his auxiliary and vicar-general, Right Rev. John M. Farley, he received a substantial proof of universal regard in the form of a legal discharge of the whole debt of the new seminary, amounting to $250,000, a testimonial initiated by Bishop Farley and by his energy and tact realized.

The Archbishop's patriotism, as the leading men of all parties knew, was of a sterling character; a warm love for his native land he carried to Europe with him in 1857 as a youth. In letters written during this journey his love for America was often expressed. When he entered the American College at Rome he was proud of the college name. Reporting the first visit of Pius IX to the college on January 29, 1860, he wrote to his family: ''You should have heard the three times three hurrahs we gave His Holiness when he praised our own Washington. The guards came running to the spot, thinking a revolution had broken out.'' On the following twenty-second of February the genial Pius IX invited the American students to an audience at the Vatican, where, after an agreeable conversation, he requested them to repeat the ''hurrah'' with which they had originally greeted him, a request that was gladly and vociferously answered. All his life long this love of country, a love that might perhaps be called a part of his religion, the Archbishop felt and displayed. Of later instances one need only recall his letter to the rectors of the diocese commending the celebration of Lafayette Day and his official action at the time of President McKinley's deplorable death.

Because of his patriotism, his moderation, his absolute non-partisanship, Archbishop Corrigan's public influence was considerable. To his representations our government listened favorably when the Italian monarchy threatened to confiscate the American College at Rome; and when obstacles were placed in the way of the proposed chapel for Catholic soldiers at West Point he was instrumental in removing them. Unfitting him for a partisan, even if the wise tradition and custom of the Church in this country had not precluded him from meddling with politics, both nature and training had fitted him for the gentler, the more becoming, the more beneficial art of diplomacy.

As an essential part of the daily round of duties, Archbishop Corrigan accounted study. A Greek scholar, a Latin, Italian, and French scholar, and, in the Seton Hall days, a close student of Hebrew, he placed first among the studious pursuits of his episcopacy those subjects in which expertness was a requisite to one who was to be a judge, an instructor, a guide, a protector, and an exemplar. Every learned work, wherever published, that could aid him to be full in front of the times—works doctrinal, moral, legal, rubrical, historical—he commanded for his library. Of every book that came to him he knew the inside. Gifted with a quick mind, he was also a rapid reader. Having a sure memory and rare powers of attention and analysis, when a volume had been finished he had absorbed and could communicate whatever in it was novel, harmful, or useful. Following continually, as he did to the end, the decisions of all the Roman Congregations, he was a veritable authority on the minute details of the manifold questions submitted to their judgment. An extensive library, well arranged, he could not help being familiar with; for he it was who placed every book on its proper shelf. On the instant, needing a volume, he could

direct whomsoever to the library section, the shelf, and even the place on the shelf. Learning, knowledge, he loved; a good book he read with eagerness. In the Scriptures, in the works of the Fathers of the Church, he was exceptionally well versed; he turned to them again and again. How constantly, unaffectedly, and yet with apparent motive he quoted from these ever flowing sources of Christian truth, his pastorals and sermons bear witness.

Versed in the classics, Greek and Latin, as well as in English, in Italian, in French, and in Spanish literature, he did not neglect contemporary work. To journals, magazines, and reviews he subscribed, reading, however, only those articles that dealt with serious questions. A novel he did not disdain when travelling.

As Bishop of Newark in 1876, as Archbishop of Petra in 1883, and as Archbishop of New York in 1890 and in 1900, he journeyed to Rome. The visit *ad limina* in 1876 was made in the company of his youngest brother, Rev. George W. Corrigan, who, having been ordained by Bishop Corrigan in the college chapel of Seton Hall on August 15, 1874, had meantime taught Greek, as well as the Evidences of the Christian Religion, in that institution. On the way to the Holy City, and returning, the Bishop visited many places that were still unknown to him. We shall mention only those to which he was led by motives of piety: Monte Cassino, reminiscent of St. Benedict and of St. Scholastica; St. Anthony's Padua, St. Catherine's and St. Bernardine's Siena, the Blessed Virgin Mary's Loretto, Venice of all the saints; Annecy, home of St. Francis de Sales; Lourdes, and then Spain, Monserrat, Manresa, Burgos, Madrid, Toledo, Cordova, with the holy week in Seville and the king and queen among the worshippers. In 1890 his companion was

Rev. Charles E. McDonnell, D.D., then his secretary and, since 1892, the bishop of the diocese of Brooklyn. Absent from the eighteenth of January to the tenth of September, he made a pilgrimage to the Holy Land first, and then, leaving Rome in June and going by Trent, over the Brenner, he visited Innspruck, Munich, Oberammergau, Prague, and Breslau. At the shrine of Einsiedeln he halted on the way to Paris. With Scotland and with the north of Ireland he made an acquaintance also before taking the steamer for home. The journey of 1900, made with his secretary, Rev. James N. Connolly, began on April 22, 1900, and ended in August of the same year. From Rome he travelled to Milan, Piacenza, Treviso; to Oberammergau a second time, and to Einsiedeln; to Paray-le-Monial; to St. Gallen; to Lourdes once again; to Meaux, to Paris, London, Oxford, Dublin, Maynooth. Where devotion did not carry him on these journeys, duty was the motor. In the archdiocese of New York there are nationalities within nationalities. To care for them all is obligatory, and the task is arduous. Communicating personally with ecclesiastical authorities in many lands, Archbishop Corrigan sought to assure a supply of zealous priests and to establish closer lines of communication.

In 1886 the spiritual care of the Bahama Islands was transferred from the see of Charleston to the see of New York, and therefore, beginning with January, 1887, every three years a visit was paid to Nassau, N. P.—a visit made by the Archbishop himself, except in 1899, when Mgr. Farley replaced him. At Nassau, besides administering confirmation, he gave the week's time to visiting the little churches and schools, to encouraging the good Benedictines and the generous Sisters of Charity who care for the small flock, and to instructing as well as to gladdening the simple colored folk, old and young.

On all the journeys, wherever made, thanks to his letters and diaries, it is possible to follow the Archbishop day by day. Until 1891 he corresponded faithfully and most agreeably with one or another of his three brothers, Rev. James H., Rev. George W., and Joseph F. Corrigan, M.D. In 1890, Rev. James H. Corrigan dying, the only two brothers left were all the more thoughtfully favored. When at home his personal correspondence was extensive, and it grew with the years. A rapid writer and sure, his written work astonishes one. Though nature had not favored him with a strong voice, he was from his priesthood a constant preacher. On the first Sunday of each month he stood in his cathedral pulpit; in other churches he spoke frequently, as he did at ordinations or consecrations, at synods, at the conferences of the clergy, in convents, at commencements, at marriages, at lay meetings, not to mention the many addresses delivered at civil gatherings. From first to last, all these addresses, speeches, sermons were carefully written before delivery. Speaking, he used no manuscript; but invariably he wrote beforehand, no matter how inconsiderable the occasion, in order to fix his thought in the most orderly fashion and to ensure precision in the language. Corrections in the manuscript were few. As in Newark, so in New York, he was industrious in editing church records; and here, as there, he had with his own hand made a list and a sketch of all the priests of the diocese from the beginning—a list that has been in part published in the "Catholic Historical Magazine."

Remarkable tributes were paid to the character and virtue of Archbishop Corrigan after his death. The action of the Holy Father was significant of the exceptionally high place he held in the esteem of the most venerable, erudite, and sagacious Pontiff. A renowned prelate of the American Church who, as far back as 1888, pronounced him to be "a perfect ecclesiast," did not hesitate now to use the word "saintly" when mourning. Other venerable bishops have repeated the word. The term "ascetic," owing to the defects of imperfect education, is too often used contemptuously, though no man wholly unascetic can be either decent or healthful, and still less can he be godly. That training of the body and of the will, that control of the passions and emotions, that exercise of the intellect in high and noble thought, that disciplined communion with Heaven, that fortitude, patience, forgiveness, gentleness, joyousness, which the ascete daily, nay hourly, strives for, Archbishop Corrigan sought from his youth to attain. The notes of his retreat for the priesthood, the notes of his meditations in Rome after his ordination—notes of reflections made in his leisure hours, his daily walks, and then committed carefully to writing—the notes of his retreat before his consecration as Bishop of Newark, were they printed here, would demonstrate how steadfastly he pursued to the end the ideals of early manhood. The life of a seminarian which he lived as a priest, he lived as bishop and archbishop. Rising at or before daybreak, his meditation made, his Mass said, the appointed portion of the office recited, from that time until the fixed hours for sleep, excepting only the too often begrudged interruption of the simple meals, he was a willing laborer. A simple member of the Diocesan Union of Priests, who freely endeavor to perform the daily devotions with regularity, he was a member who rarely had to report any neglect. At the annual retreats of the clergy he was one of themselves. To the Blessed Virgin Mary his attachment was amiably fervent. The visit he made to Mexico in 1895 with the Right Rev. Bishop Farley and with the Rev. James N. Connolly, his trusty secretary, will be remembered—

a visit to the shrine of Our Lady of Guadalupe, under whose patronage the American College students commenced their first retreat. To the Sacred Heart of Jesus he consecrated solemnly the diocese of Newark in 1873, and at his request the feast was created a Double of the Second Class. People and clergy he urged to be more than ever mindful of the Passion of Our Divine Lord in Lent. Of the many titles by which the loving devotion of Catholics to the Virgin Mother of God is figured he favored especially one—Our Lady of Good Counsel. In New York, as in Newark, he named in her honor the first church built in either diocese after his installation. A member of the third order of St. Francis of Assisi he was professed, in the Church of St. John the Baptist, West Thirtieth street, New York City, by Rev. Lawrence Vorwerk, on January 30, 1887. To erudition, industry, tact, decision; to the supernatural aid of his patrons, the forceful Archangel Michael and the contrite Doctor, Augustine, the Archbishop of New York was careful to add, when proud men threatened, an appeal to him who was proud in being ''a fool for Christ's sake.''

Among the Archbishop's devotions we have not named the first—devotion to the Most Blessed Sacrament of the Altar. Seeking the Sisters of St. Dominic in their convent near Lyons, France, while on the visit *ad limina* in 1876, he made arrangements for the foundation of a convent in Newark, to be dedicated to the Perpetual Adoration of the Most Blessed Sacrament. Overcoming many obstacles, the convent was at length opened in 1880. The altar, donated by himself, was consecrated in 1884, and at this altar he said his farewell Mass in the city of Newark. Coming to New York, he was intent upon founding a similar convent there. Only in 1889 was his desire fulfilled, when the Monastery of Corpus Christi was established at

Hunt's Point, in charge of the Dominican Sisters and governed by the Superior, an American, who had organized the Newark institution. In October, 1900, the Archbishop, introducing into the centre of the city the Fathers of the Congregation of the Most Blessed Sacrament, still further incited his flock to piety, while seeking increased blessings upon the diocese through this new sanctuary of Perpetual Adoration.

At Milan, at Annecy, we have seen the Archbishop. To these memorable sites his two foremost episcopal models drew him: the meek St. Francis de Sales, "who studied as much at the foot of the crucifix as in books"; and St. Charles Borromeo, " the model of pastors and the reformer of ecclesiastical discipline." Following the one, he could not help being a pupil of the other. As St. Charles conscientiously applied the law of the Council of Trent, so Bishop Corrigan and Archbishop Corrigan endeavored to make effective all the decrees of the Councils of Baltimore. Of his fidelity to the cause of Catholic education in the archdiocese, so world-wide did his critics insist on proclaiming and declaiming it, we have said no more than to quote figures showing the increase of parochial schools during his rule. And yet here we cannot pass over his address to the clergy in the last synod he held—an address pointedly reaffirming the decrees of the third plenary council of Baltimore.

On the eve of the feast of the Dedication of St. Michael, in the year 1884, the Archbishop of Petra, residing then in the same house with Cardinal McCloskey, received a message from the venerable Cardinal asking an interview—an invitation that was promptly answered. An attendant on the Cardinal had, by his direction, selected from a private drawer the Pectoral Cross most valued by His Eminence. When Archbishop Corrigan had entered the prelate's room, the Cardinal said to him:

"To-morrow will be your feast day. I desire to make you a little present. I now present this cross to the most humble man I have ever known." There are laymen living who often thought of saying aloud what the aged, the experienced, the reticent Cardinal so generously and beautifully said. The cross handed to the Archbishop of Petra was one that, having been the property of Archbishop Hughes, had, after his death, passed into the possession of his sister, who was then the Mother Superior at the Academy of Mount St. Vincent on the Hudson. She it was who presented it to the Cardinal. The Bishop of Rochester, preaching at the consecration of the Bishop of Newark in 1873, had poetically indicated his lowliness of mind. Nigh thirty years distant from that day, Cardinal Ledochowski, hearing of the Archbishop's death, described him as " the most solid column of the Church in America," and as one who had been " the most humble and the most just of men."

From the diaries, letters, sermons of Michael Augustine Corrigan one could fill pages exhibiting his admiration of the virtue of humility, and his constant effort to cultivate the virtue in himself by guarding himself against the temptations to pride that office and honor and even sincere praise induce.

Together with humility, he cherished a habit without which the highest virtue is unfruitful, if, indeed, it be possible. From a charming canticle on Divine Love, attributed by some critics to St. Francis of Assisi, and by others to one of his early disciples, Dante Rossetti has reverently translated the words that Christ speaks to a loving soul:

> Set Love in order, thou that lovest Me.
> Never was virtue out of order found;
> And though I fill thy heart desirously,
> By thine own virtue I must keep My ground:

When to My love thou dost bring charity,
Even she must come with order girt and gown'd.
 Look how the trees are bound
 To order, bearing fruit;
 And by one thing compute,
In all things earthly, order's grace or gain.

All earthly things I had the making of
Were numbered and were measured then by Me;
And each was ordered to its end by Love,
Each kept, through order, clean for ministry.
Charity most of all, when known enough,
Is of her very nature orderly.
 Lo now! what heat in thee,
 Soul, can have bred this rout?
 Thou putt'st all order out.
Even this love's heat must be its curb and rein.

In charity, as in all things else, Michael Augustine Corrigan aimed at order. In orderliness lay the secret of his doing and of his eminence. Habit grew to be nature. Gentle, too, was this spirit of order. Ever visible, no one associated with the Archbishop was incommoded by its presence. Chiding never, never constraining, it was none the less efficient—by example. Thanks to this spirit of order, this virtue of order, he worthily earned the eulogy of the prudent and discerning Apostolic Delegate, Cardinal Martinelli, a holy man himself,—one experienced in men and in ecclesiastical affairs,—who, leaving our land, said of him: "The Archbishop of New York was a man of great learning and eminent piety, with a mind moulded to advance the welfare of the Church by precept and by practice. His loss to the Church is grievous. He was conservative, and he has left behind him institutions of great value, whose usefulness will be progressive with the age."

JOHN A. MOONEY.

THE OBSEQUIES

–

St. Patrick's Cathedral

New York

THE OBSEQUIES

The Rev. James N. Connolly

FORMERLY SECRETARY TO THE ARCHBISHOP

THE body of his Grace the Most Reverend Archbishop was removed from the room wherein he died, to the west parlor, and after it was dressed according to the prescriptions of the Ritual in the pontifical vestments it was laid on a high, black-covered bier. A small crucifix was in his joined hands, a white damask mitre was placed on his head, and the pallium, the distinctive emblem of archiepiscopal rank, with its three stone-set pins, fell across his shoulders. Candles were set at the head and foot of the catafalque, and a small table with a book, candles, and holy water was placed near it. At the foot of the bier was the episcopal green silk-corded hat.

The general public was not allowed to enter the house, but there was a continuous stream of nuns entering all the day to look for the last time upon their spiritual father, and to offer at his feet a fervent prayer for his happy repose.

On Wednesday morning the remains were carried in solemn procession to the Cathedral by the Right Rev. Mgr. Edwards and the Rev. Fathers McGean, McCready, Phelan, Flood, and Colton.

On leaving the archiepiscopal residence the procession turned to the right, through Fiftieth Street, to Fifth Avenue, and then into the Cathedral by the main portal. The deep tones of the great bell in the tower announced to all that the

51

chief shepherd of the flock was being borne on the shoulders of his beloved priests to the majestic Cathedral he had done so much to beautify.

Arriving at the elevated catafalque which had been especially constructed to receive his remains, the body of the Archbishop was raised up and placed in an inclined position, with his face turned toward the thousands of mourners who were anxious to look again upon his saintly countenance and to join in the prayers for his eternal repose.

At the head a large cluster of unbleached wax candles were lighted, and the episcopal hat was placed at the foot.

The Rev. George W. Corrigan; Dr. Joseph F. Corrigan, with his children; Father D. J. Curley, the secretary of the Archbishop; and the attendants of the archiepiscopal household, who were in the procession and walked immediately behind the corpse, took seats in the church near the catafalque.

When the long line of clergy had taken their places in the sanctuary, the solemn recital of the Office of the Dead was begun. The absolutions were given at the end of each Nocturn, and after the chanting of Lauds the Right Rev. Bishop McQuaid gave the last absolution.

When the versicles and prayers had been sung the clergy retired, and the final arrangements at and around the catafalque were then made. A guard composed of prominent Catholic laymen of the city, under the direction of a special committee of the Catholic Club, together with a detail from the Sixty-ninth Regiment of the National Guard, took their places about the catafalque and were in attendance all the time until the funeral services were ended on Friday morning.

The public were then allowed to pass by the catafalque, and from that moment until the day of the interment a continual

stream of people, of all classes and of all walks of life, poured
into the Cathedral. It may truly be said that no such throngs
of men, women, and children ever viewed the body of an
American prelate lying in state, as passed by the bier on which
rested all that was mortal of New York's metropolitan.

Many evidences there were that Archbishop Corrigan had
endeared himself during life not only to his own flock, but to
thousands of others who, in many ways, had come under his
benign influence. He was known to them as the saintly priest,
the unassuming prelate, the encouraging adviser, the true
father, the kind and thoughtful friend. Many a tear that
started from the moistened eyes of even those who were not of
his own fold, but who had come to look upon his face once more
and to give evidence of their respect and reverence for him,
was occasioned by the remembrances of his acts of kindness to
them. The hand of death had put a stop to his good deeds on
earth, but it could not stay the deep feelings of love, of affection, and of gratitude which manifested themselves on all sides.
The people had thought they knew him, but it was only when he
was stricken down that they began to realize that they had not
appreciated to the full what a noble bishop they had had to rule
them, what a bright example he had daily set them, what a
saintly man had walked among them.

On Wednesday evening the solemn Office of the Dead was
again chanted. The sanctuary was filled with priests and seminarians. The levites from Dunwoodie joined their youthful
voices with those of their elders in prayerful supplication for
him whose whole life had been spent for his people.

On Friday morning at ten o'clock the Pontifical Mass of Requiem was begun. As the great bell began to toll, the clergy,
who had vested in the Boland School on Madison Avenue,

began the procession to the Cathedral. It may be safely said
that on the streets of no other city in the world, at the present
day, could such a sight have been witnessed. There was first a
long line of distinguished Catholic laymen, members of the
Catholic Club, and many representatives of all the different
Catholic societies of men in the diocese. Then came the young
clerics, one hundred and fifty in number, from Dunwoodie
Seminary, walking two by two, and dressed in cassock, sur-
plice, and beretta. Following them came the representatives
of the various religious orders. There were Augustinians,
Augustinians of the Assumption, Benedictines, Capuchins,
Carmelites, Dominicans, Franciscans, Jesuits, Fathers of
Mercy, Fathers of the Pious Society of Missions, Missionaries
of St. Charles, Missionaries of St. Paul the Apostle, Re-
demptorists, Salesians, Sulpicians, Brothers of the Christian Schools, and Marist Brothers. These were in turn
followed by the secular priests of the diocese, and their numbers were augmented by clergy from many parts of the United
States and Canada. There were young and old in the line,
and types of almost every nation and people on the earth.
Thousands of persons, who had given up all hope of gaining
admission into the church, crowded all the surrounding streets
and avenues, and it required a double line of soldiers and po-
lice to make room for the march of this grand army of priests.
The general good order which is characteristic of New York,
especially when large crowds are gathered together, prevailed
throughout the day. The city journals commented on this fact,
so noticeable was the decorum and composure of the multitude.
It was not a gathering of idle curiosity-seekers. It was the
spontaneous outpouring of the city's people to show respect
to the dead. All wished to enter the great church, but all could

not, and so those without were content to stand in respectful silence as the procession went by, and to take as much part as they could in the service.

As the last of the priests passed by the Archbishop's house, the bishops and archbishops, in rochette and mantelletta, and his Eminence the Cardinal Archbishop of Baltimore, in cappa magna, joined them.

The guard of honor from the Sixty-ninth Regiment, stationed on the outside of the church, saluted the prelates as they entered. The high portals of the Cathedral were draped in black and purple, and the mournful colors surrounding the massive columns of the interior brought out in bolder relief the exquisite lines of the vaulted roof and clerestory. The white marble altar at the eastern end was unadorned. Six unbleached wax candles, three on either side of the crucifix, were burning. The sanctuary floor was entirely covered with purple cloth, and the vacant throne of the third Archbishop of New York was festooned with black and purple hangings.

The celebrant of the Mass was his Eminence James Cardinal Gibbons, Archbishop of Baltimore. The Right Rev. Monsignor Joseph F. Mooney was the assistant priest. The Right Rev. Monsignor John Edwards and the Rev. Charles H. Colton were the deacons of honor. The deacon of the Mass was the Rev. James H. McGean, and the subdeacon, the Rev. Michael J. Lavelle. The Revs. James N. Connolly and Thomas F. Myhan were the masters of ceremonies. There were present archbishops, bishops, mitred abbots, monsignori, and nearly one thousand priests. It was estimated that there were from six thousand to seven thousand people in the Cathedral. Three times as many more were in the plazas surrounding the church and on the sidewalks in Fifth and Madison avenues and Fiftieth and Fifty-first streets. The demands for tickets of admission reached over fifty thousand.

Seated in prominent places in the church were the mayor of the city, and representatives of the different departments of the city government, as well as of the Supreme Court. There were also many other city, State, and Federal officials present. At the foot of the catafalque was a touching evidence of the esteem of the chief magistrate of the country for the dead prelate. It was a wreath of flowers sent from the White House, with a simple card attached—"The President."

Seldom, indeed, is such an assemblage witnessed. The civil and religious honors shown the dead Archbishop were unusual. It is more than rare to find under one roof at the same time such a complex gathering, from the little orphan children and the humble poor to the most exalted in church and state, including even many of those who were teachers in other folds.

There was no doubt but that a great man had died, and it was more than evident that the noble efforts of his life had been justly appreciated and acknowledged.

The Gregorian chant of the chancel choir and the figured music of the large choir most feelingly interpreted the mind of the Church and the thoughts of the silent throng of worshippers. At the end of the Mass the Most Rev. P. J. Ryan, Archbishop of Philadelphia, ascended the pulpit and delivered the oration over the dead.

Archbishop Ryan   Archbishop Corrigan

Third Plenary Council of Baltimore, 1885

ARCHBISHOP RYAN'S EULOGY OF HIS DEAD FRIEND

Venerable Fathers, dear brethren of the laity:

BEHOLD a great priest who in his day pleased God and was found just; behold him in the vestments of his order as he stood at that altar to offer sacrifice and prayers for you and yours; behold him who but a few days ago spoke from this pulpit of truth those great doctrines that are to save society from socialism and anarchy, and who now, being dead, yet speaketh from that funeral pulpit by the eloquence of his past life. Behold the cardinal and his brother bishops are here, to do him honor who was the example to us of every episcopal virtue. His priests are here, both secular and regular, they who had so many opportunities to look into his heart, and knew that every fibre of it breathed the sacerdotal spirit; and the Christian Brothers, the representatives of that Christian education of which he was the fearless defender—they are here to receive new inspiration in their great work; and you—you spouses of Jesus Christ, you gentle Sisterhoods of every order and of every work of charity—you are assembled around his bier to offer the tribute of your prayers and your tears; to look for the last time into the face of your dead Father and friend; and you—you his people, the people in whose heart is ever enshrined the memory of the true priest and the true bishop, the sheep who know the shepherd; you, who by an intuition of faith will find out, though you may be deceived for a time, who

was the real bishop—you are here around his coffin; and you
of whom the Lord hath said, "and other sheep I have that are
not of this fold"—you are here because you know the advantage to a great community such as New York, of a character like that of the late Archbishop, the influence of that
character for truth, for order, for disinterestedness—you are
here to show your appreciation of him. But what can I say in
such surroundings? How can I, how can any man translate
into words the thoughts of the mind, the emotions of the heart
that must well up in an environment like this?

But, my dear brethren, we are not here to-day merely to
honor the memory of the dead Archbishop. We are here to do
that, but not that alone. A Sacrifice has been offered on that
altar—not a Mass of thanksgiving for his achievements, not a
commemoration of him and all his deeds—no; that awful Sacrifice was offered that God might have mercy on his soul; that
pure Host, that holy Host, that Immaculate Host, that Bread
of Eternal Life and Chalice of Everlasting Salvation, Him by
Whom and in Whom are offered to the omnipotent Father in
the unity of the Holy Ghost all honor and glory, offered whilst
Angels praise and Dominations adore and Powers tremble;
that Sacrifice was offered, that God might have mercy on him.
Strange words—mercy on him, whose childhood, whose boyhood, whose seminary life, whose priestly life, whose episcopal
life, was so pure, so beautiful—but yet, O God! how awful is
Thy sanctity! Yet, because of the responsibilities of his station, because nothing defiled, in great or little, shall pass the
portals of eternal life; therefore we meet to ask God to have
mercy on his soul. From that bier he might this morning cry
out to us: "Not praise, but pity have on me. At least, you my
friends, you my people, you my priests, you my brother

bishops, have pity on me, for the hand of the Lord hath touched me with purifying touch.'' No matter how slight may be the imperfection, that imperfection must be atoned for before heaven can be entered.

There are those who think that the Catholic Church unduly exalts her pastors and the chief of pastors above the people, that the pastors may rule them, that they may have influence with them. But, no; the Church loses not sight of personal responsibility amidst the splendors of office. That Sovereign Pontiff who to-day is borne through the Basilica of St. Peter's and seems almost a demigod as he opens his hand and fills every living creature with his benediction, he who is worshipped almost as a demigod, will to-morrow be seen at the feet of some poor priest, striking his breast and saying, ''Bless me, Father, for I have sinned, through my fault, through my fault, through my most grievous fault; I ask of thee absolution and penance.'' So, whilst the office is exalted, the man is humbled. And should that Sovereign Pontiff depart from us, a service like this will be offered that God might have mercy on him because of the account that He will demand of him. So, brethren, not alone to praise but to pray are we met to-day.

With regard to the merits of the deceased: his biography has been published in all the journals of the day, and it is not necessary that I should rehearse it here, edifying as it might be. The world can speak only of external achievements, outward actions. They are not enough for great merit. Bold, strong, and vicious men have done great things in their day, from unworthy motives. God regards not their work. It is the greatness of goodness that is important. They who act from vainglorious motives will soon be forgotten even by men, for the world knows its own weakness and mutability, and does honor only to the magnanimity that despises its vain praise. The permanently great are those who act from higher motives. The inner life, the life hidden in God, the life of pure intentions, the life of self-sacrifice, producing great actions— this is the life that is truly great. We often hear men of the world say nowadays: "The age of merely ascetic bishops and priests has passed away. Asceticism did well enough in the Middle Ages. We want the stirring, public man." But the truth is, brethren, we want both, the combination of both, the combination of the ascetic with the public man, but the larger element of asceticism in that combination. Such was the departed Archbishop of New York. Sufficiently of the world, yet in that inner life, in that sense of the presence of God, in that purity of intention, in that restrained force, he attracted public men, who will not misjudge. There is something in a real man, with true manhood and, added to that, spiritual manhood—there is something in nearness to Jesus Christ that attracts men as He Himself attracted them. There is something in the priesthood of our Lord that attracts even the worst, for the worst men have yet good in them. They are won by genuine virtue, and admire it in others even though they do not possess it themselves.

His aim was to act purely for God and for his fellow-men, not to please, but to displease when necessary, but always to benefit. Hence his life of marvellous labor. It was wonderful how much this one man did. The people see only the public acts, but his daily life, his anxieties, his labors in silence, the world did not heed, and all these labors he undertook and discharged with a boyish enthusiasm. Some one has said, that enthusiasm belongs only to youth, and the aged and the grave should not be enthusiastic. No; enthusiasm is born of motive. The young, fired by the ambition to be great, to love, and, higher still, to aid their fellow-men by pure philanthropy, they are enthusiastic until the ends are attained. When love is satiated, when ambition is disappointed, when philanthropy is chilled by the ingratitude of those benefited, enthusiasm dies. But he who works for God, as God cannot die, and divine love cannot be satiated—for many waters cannot quench it, and floods cannot drown it—when men act for their fellow-men for God's sake, the motive continues and the enthusiasm is perennial. Tertullian, in the second century, speaking of old men amongst the early priesthood, called them boys, boys in their enthusiasm, boys in their love for God, boys in the motive that nerved them with the freshness, the self-sacrifice, the beauty, the intensity of youth in their old age, because the motive remained perennial.

The three Archbishops of this see represented three features of human character. The Most Rev. John Hughes represented courage, invincible courage, at a time, too, when it was needed. Cardinal McCloskey represented marvellous prudence that won without fighting. The late Archbishop might be regarded as belonging to the class of Cardinal McCloskey, yet, when a principle was at stake, the lamb became a lion, and he was found fearless as ever was Archbishop Hughes. *Dominus petra mea*, the Lord is my rock: because he leaned upon God, because he knew his motives were supernatural, he worked with the inspired intrepidity of God. *Dominus petra mea* was the motto of Moses the meek, and Moses the unconquerable. The Archbishop was himself as a rock, gentle, yielding, mossy on the surface; but beneath all that gentleness strength and power and immovability of principle were found.

The late Cardinal McCloskey told me that Archbishop Corrigan did all that he could that his name should not be sent to Rome as coadjutor with right of succession to this see. He was afraid of its responsibilities. So the greatest bishops that ever lived were afraid of the responsibilities of the episcopate, and because they were afraid they were great, but when they were obliged to accept, they became the bravest. St. Ambrose hid himself lest he should be made Bishop of Milan. Yet St. Ambrose faced the master of the world at the portals of his own cathedral. He faced the Roman Emperor, Theodosius the Great, and he said to his very face, "I will not admit thee to the sanctuary of God until thou hast done penance for thy sins." The Roman Emperor in the Roman Empire dared by one of his own subjects! This Emperor deserved the title of great, not only because of his achievements in battle, but because he knew when to submit, and the fearless but apparently timid bishop said to him, "David had sinned and was received. Thou who didst imitate David in his sin go and imitate David in his penance and then I shall admit thee."

So with Thomas à Becket, so with the great bishops who desired not the dignity and were apparently timid, but became great with the greatness and courage that God communicated to them. "No man has dared to speak to me," said the pagan magistrate to St. Basil; "no man has dared to speak to me as thou hast." "Perhaps," said the Bishop, "it is because thou hast never met a Christian Bishop." In that combination of modesty, humility and moral courage is the perfection of the man and the priest and the bishop, because they are modelled on our Divine Lord, Who was perfect humanity. How gentle He was. How humble. He washed the feet of His apostles. He washed the feet of Judas Iscariot; yet when the time came for the exercise of power and authority, how He scourged the buyers and sellers from the Temple of God, how He claimed

the right of His office, how He said to His apostles whose feet
He washed, "You call me Lord and Master, and you do right,
for so I am." How He vindicated His dignity, how He became
the model of the bishop, kind, tender, affectionate, self-sacrificing, bold, strong in the discharge of His great duties!

A newspaper of this city of high literary standing has said
of the late Archbishop that as the perfume of the virtues of St.
Francis of Assisium still remains amongst men after so many
centuries, so also shall the perfume of the virtues of Archbishop Corrigan survive amongst his people. Oh, the impress
of such a character, its effect, the love that it will call out will
grow with time. Men who did not acknowledge it will acknowledge it as time passes by. The little children will remember it.
Oh, what is death to such a man as this! What a liberation,
an illumination, a union! A liberation from the trials and suf-
ferings and responsibilities of this life; an illumination when
he shall look into the very face of God and be made like unto
Him. "We shall be like unto Him for we shall see Him as He
is." So the apostle declares. It is an illumination by which he
will see the length and breadth and height and depth of God's
love. The problems of human life shall be solved for him, the
illumination of intellect, the touching of hearts. "Oh, when
wilt Thou take me to Thyself, O Spouse?" said St. Peter of
Alcantara, and "When shall I be dissolved and be with
Christ?" said the apostle of the Gentiles.

O God, Thou Who didst give such graces to Thy servant,
grant that we, who are left a little while longer, only a little
while, may imitate his virtues, that we may be united to him
in eternal life, through Christ our Lord. Amen.

At the close of the sermon the preparations were begun for
the five solemn absolutions.

When the Supreme Pontiff, a cardinal, a metropolitan, or a bishop of a diocese dies there are five absolutions performed over his remains at the end of the Mass of Requiem. In other cases there is but one absolution. These five absolutions were given in turn by Bishops McQuaid of Rochester, Ludden of Syracuse, Gabriels of Ogdensburg, and Burke of Albany, and by his Eminence the Cardinal,—all attired in copes and mitres. The four bishops took their respective places at the corners of the bier, and his Eminence sat facing the crucifix which was held by the subdeacon, with acolytes on either side of him, at the head of the catafalque.

The celebrant read the opening prayer and then each bishop in turn, as soon as the responsories had been sung by the chancel choir, encircled the remains, blessing with holy water and incensing. The fifth and final absolution was administered by the Cardinal. During this long and impressive ceremony the vast congregation remained standing. When the little surpliced orphans, whose new home their dead benefactor had all but opened to them, had shrilled out the last "Requiescat in pace," the "Amen" rose instinctively to the lips of all; and with that deep, suspended feeling of emotion which only such surroundings could evoke, the long procession quietly wended its way out of the Cathedral.

When all had withdrawn from the church preparations were made for the final interment. A death-mask of the prelate was taken by Mr. Joseph Sibbel, the sculptor, and the body, just as it had been exposed to view, was lifted into the coffin. After the Archbishop's brothers and relatives had taken a last farewell, a white linen cloth was placed over the mouth, and a sealed glass bottle containing a sheet of parchment on which was written the name and a short history of the Archbishop was enclosed, and the lid was placed over the remains of one of

the great champions of God's Church. The inscription on the
lid was surmounted by a cross and read as follows:

MICHAEL AUGUSTINUS CORRIGAN
ARCHIEPISCOPUS NEO-EBORACENSIS TERTIUS

NATUS NOVARCI DIE 13 AUGUSTI A.D. 1839

PRESBYTER DIE 19 SEPTEMBRIS A.D. 1863

EPISCOPUS NOVARCENSIS DIE 4 MAII A.D. 1873

ARCHIEPISCOPUS PETRENSIS ET COADJUTOR NEO-EBORACENSIS

DIE 1 OCTOBRIS A.D. 1880

ARCHIEPISCOPUS NEO-EBORACENSIS DIE 10 OCTOBRIS A.D. 1885

OBIIT DIE 5 MAII A.D. 1902

Those present formed in procession to the chamber in the
crypt under the sanctuary, and after the prayers of interment
had been read by the venerable Dean of the Province of New
York, the Right Rev. Bishop McQuaid, the body was put in a
metal-lined casket which was then placed in a niche alongside
the remains of his predecessors, Cardinal McCloskey and Archbishop Hughes. The chamber was closed with a marble slab
which bore an inscription in Latin. Above the inscription was
a cross, and below it the coat of arms of Archbishop Corrigan.
The inscription is as follows:

MICHAEL AUGUSTINUS CORRIGAN
SOLIO PONTIFICIO ASSISTENS

ARCHIEPISCOPUS NEO-EBORACENSIS TERTIUS

ANNO MDCCCLXXXV RENUNCIATUS

CHRISTIANAE INSTITUTIONIS INVICTUS ASSERTOR

VIXIT AN. LXIII

OBIIT DIE V MAII MCMII

SIT IN PACE LOCUS EJUS.

MICHAEL AUGUSTINE CORRIGAN
ASSISTANT AT THE PONTIFICAL THRONE
THIRD ARCHBISHOP OF NEW YORK
THE STAUNCH DEFENDER OF CHRISTIAN EDUCATION
DIED MAY 5TH, 1902
MAY HIS PLACE BE IN PEACE.

THE VOICES OF FRIENDS

Archbishop Corrigan

Rome, 1890

EULOGY OF THE LATE ARCHBISHOP

By Rev. Henry A. Brann, D.D.

AT THE AMERICAN COLLEGE ALUMNI MEETING

Mr. President and Brother Alumni:

IT is hard for me to control my emotions when I have to speak on this theme; to speak of the character and virtues of my old schoolmate and lifelong cherished friend, the dead Archbishop of New York. I knew him long, well, and intimately. The specific attribute of Archbishop Corrigan was his piety. This was the center from which all his other qualities and all his actions radiated. His piety made him a man of tender conscience. No one could understand him perfectly while he lived, and no one can understand him properly now that he is dead, who did not and who does not measure him and his acts by the standard of conscience enlightened and regulated by law.

Long before the American College at Rome existed he was my classmate in an American college at home; and there he was the white lily of all the flowers in the garden. In Rome he was the Aloysius of the Levites of the sanctuary; and as a priest, bishop, and archbishop the whiteness of his life was unstained, and the fragrance of his virtues was universally diffused. If all prayed as he did there would be no critics of his character. Piety was the sweet dominant note in the oratorio of his life.

His piety inspired the application which made him also a

69

great scholar. We have had among our alumni men of more brilliant parts and men who excelled him in special studies, but none equaled him in thorough comprehension of the encyclopedia of ecclesiastical science. He conscientiously and persistently cultivated his well-endowed and well-balanced mind to the very end of his life. The venerable Bishop of Rochester told me that Dr. Corrigan, when professor at Seton Hall, studied eight hours a day. He knew the matter of all the theologies and of Canon Law and of the Holy Scriptures, and he knew also the form in which to give adequate expression to his knowledge. No one did more than he in the last Council of Baltimore to suggest, shape, and mould the decrees which are to-day the rules of conduct and discipline of the clergy in the United States. He was an indefatigable worker from his boyhood to his grave. Although never strong or sturdy, he did the work of a vigorous man. In him intelligence, informed by truth, illuminated and dominated by the idea of duty, ruled with inexorable sway. His intellect, endowed by grace, made him methodical, precise, careful, correct, and cautious. He crossed every *t* and dotted every *i*. From the early morning watch until late at night all his actions were guided by rule; and in spite of the variety and multiplicity of his occupations and distractions as priest, bishop, and archbishop, he was as regular in the discharge of his spiritual duties as a fervent seminarian. When his frail body flagged, his soul spurred and whipped it into action, making every fiber and muscle work in the service of his Divine Master. All knew this; and therefore when, under the strain of worry caused by constant annoyance, anxiety, and overwork, the crows' feet began to gather around his tired eyes and his brain and heart began to show the effects of the strain, no one was surprised.

The late Vicar-General Preston, himself a man of parts, who had enjoyed the intimacy of the first two archbishops of New York, the Lion of the Fold of Judah and the magnetic Fénelon of our Church, said of Archbishop Corrigan: "This one is the equal and in some respects the superior of all."

Although the Archbishop was impulsive by temperament, his piety held his impulses in check. He bore no resentment. He fostered no dislikes. He forgave easily. The facts which prove this are so well known that they need not be enumerated. His battles were not of his seeking. He shrank from conflict; but when discipline or faith required it, his conscience raised the flag and his achievements followed it to the end.

In the great fight for Catholic education he simply repeated the cry of faith of Pius IX; the battle-cry of all the popes from Peter to Leo the Illuminator: "Non possumus." No man ever lived more loyal or devoted to the great Pontiff and the See of Peter. When the ripples of recent controversies shall have disappeared from the sea on which the bark of Peter is always breasting the waves and the storms, some historian of the future, studying the acts and circumstances of Michael Augustine Corrigan's life in detail, will portray his character in all its beauteous colors, and place him in the galaxy where Bruté and Dubois, Newman and England, the Kenricks and Spalding, McCloskey and Hughes, are shining in the splendors of scholarly fame, apostolic zeal, and angelic sanctity.

MONSIGNOR DOANE'S TRIBUTE TO
ARCHBISHOP CORRIGAN

(FROM THE " NEW YORK TRIBUNE " OF THE SEVENTH OF MAY)

" To the Editor of the ' Tribune ':

" Sir, I have just finished reading your notice of Archbishop Corrigan, whose death, so much to be deplored, occurred last night. In many respects you do him full justice, but there is one point upon which you have but slightly touched, and that is the loveliness of his character and the charm of his relations with others. He seemed to walk in the footsteps of Fénelon and St. Francis de Sales. I have known him nearly fifty years, and used to say that at one time he was a parishioner of mine, since, as a young man, I used to see him in his father's pew in the Cathedral.

" When he went to Europe I gave him a letter of introduction to Dom Bernardo Smith, afterward Abbot Smith, the Benedictine professor at the Propaganda in Rome. After his return we were much thrown together while Bishop Bayley was still here.

" While he was Bishop of Newark, I was his Vicar-General, and daily in consultation with him at a time when much was done in the growth of the diocese, especially in the establishment of the religious communities, such as the Sisters of the Good Shepherd, the Little Sisters of the Poor, and the Dominican Nuns. Anybody more laborious and methodical in

72

his work could not be conceived. He was ' totus in illis,' and, to speak with reverence, always about his ' Father's business.'

" His promotion to New York never, to use a common expression, ' turned a hair.' He remained the same humble, affable, painstaking, spiritual-minded man he had always been. In this sense, when I have been with him in the beautiful resi- dence that he occupied next the Cathedral, I have often admired him when I noticed that with all the influence and power and position that his high office gave him, he was as Archbishop Corrigan just as simple, sweet, and modest and unassuming as I had known him as a boy. ' The boy was father of the man.'

" Others will tell of all he has accomplished in his quiet way since he went to New York, and of the great seminary he built at Dunwoodie, and how he was preparing to consecrate the Cathedral.

" He was most delightful both as a host and as a guest, and when the bow was unbent enjoyed his recreation, enlivening the conversation with his apt remarks and his little cheery laugh, and paying the utmost attention to what was said by those about him. He was most courteous at all times to all with whom he came in contact.

" The last time I saw him was shortly after the fatal fall, when he was confined to his chair in his sitting-room. I said to him, ' You will hardly go to the prince's dinner,' and he laughingly said, ' Why, I cannot leave the room.'

" I write this from a sick-bed, as I am only just slowly recovering from a violent attack of illness, which has kept me from his side, and will prevent my going to his requiem. But at least I can offer these few heartfelt words as a tribute to his dear memory, and as a slight expression of my love and admiration and friendship for him, whose death has laid the great archdiocese low in grief, a grief that will be shared by all, far and near, who ever knew and loved him, for the two were sure to go together in every case.

> " 'None knew thee but to love thee,
> Nor named thee but to praise.'

" Eternal rest grant unto him, O Lord, and may light perpetual shine upon him! "

THE VOICE OF THE LAITY

The Most Reverend John M. Farley

Fourth Archbishop of New York

1902

THE VOICE OF THE LAITY

IN order that the laity might have an opportunity of testifying in a special manner to their appreciation of the loss they had sustained in the death of the Archbishop, a great meeting was called at Carnegie Hall, on Sunday evening, June 8, under the auspices of

THE CATHOLIC CLUB
CATHOLIC BENEVOLENT LEGION
CATHOLIC KNIGHTS OF AMERICA
CATHOLIC SINGING SOCIETIES
HOLY NAME SOCIETY
KNIGHTS OF COLUMBUS
ST. VINCENT DE PAUL SOCIETY
YOUNG MEN'S ARCHDIOCESAN UNION
XAVIER ALUMNI SODALITY

The arrangements were in charge of the following committees representing those different organized bodies of the city of New York:

GEORGE J. GILLESPIE, *Chairman*
CHARLES MURRAY, *Secretary*
General Committee of Arrangements.

COMMITTEE ON INVITATIONS

THOMAS M. MULRY, *Chairman*

MICHAEL E. BANNIN
NICHOLAS E. BENZIGER
JOHN BYRNE
LAWRENCE J. CALLANAN
FREDERICK R. COUDERT
JOHN CRANE
CORNELIUS CONKLIN
JOSEPH DILLON
DANIEL J. EARLY
JOHN DUNCAN EMMET
PAUL FULLER
FRANK T. FITZGERALD
JEREMIAH FITZPATRICK
LEONARD A. GIEGERICH
JOHN F. GIBBONS

WILLIAM R. GRACE
WILLIAM E. ISELIN
JAMES G. JOHNSON
JOHN P. KELLY
ROBERT KELLY
THOMAS LENANE
JAMES E. MCLARNEY
MARTIN T. MCMAHON
AUGUSTE P. MONTANT
JEREMIAH A. MAHONEY
JAMES J. O'BRIEN
JOSEPH E. OWENS
CORNELIUS O'REILLY
JOHN J. PULLEYN
CLARENCE J. RAMSEY

COMMITTEE ON SPEAKERS AND CEREMONIES

JOHN H. SPELLMAN, *Chairman*

WILLIAM J. AMEND
THOMAS BARRETT
MICHAEL BRENNAN
CHARLES ASTOR BRISTED
JOHN J. BARRY
JUAN M. CEBALLOS
MICHAEL COLEMAN
GEORGE B. COLEMAN
JAMES E. DOUGHERTY
JOSEPH F. DALY
THOMAS ADDIS EMMET, M.D.
JAMES R. FLOYD
JOHN FOX
HUGH J. GRANT
ISAAC A. HOPPER

THOMAS H. KELLY
MARTIN J. KEOGH
EDWARD L. KEYES, M.D.
HENRY MCALEENAN
JOHN W. MACKAY
WILLIAM P. O'CONNOR
DANIEL O'DAY
HERMAN RIDDER
GEORGE B. ROBINSON
WILLIAM SCHICKEL
PAUL L. THEBAUD
FRANCIS C. TRAVERS
RICHARD S. TREACY
AUGUSTIN WALSH
SCHUYLER N. WARREN

COMMITTEE ON FINANCE

JAMES J. PHELAN, *Chairman*

JOHN G. AGAR	HUGH KELLY
JOHN D. CRIMMINS	PETER A. LALOR
JAMES ROSS CURRAN	WILLIAM LUMMIS
PETER DOELGER	JAMES D. LYNCH
MICHAEL J. DRUMMOND	JOHN A. McCALL
GEORGE EHRET	PETER McDONNELL
PATRICK FARRELLY	GEORGE B. McGINNIS
STEPHEN FARRELLY	GEORGE D. MACKAY
THOMAS L. FEITNER	JOHN B. MANNING
CHARLES V. FORNES	THOMAS C. O'SULLIVAN
JAMES O. FARRELL	JOHN G. O'KEEFFE
HENRY HEIDE	JAMES A. O'GORMAN
FRANCIS HIGGINS	EUGENE A. PHILBIN
ROBERT J. HOGUET	THOMAS F. RYAN
ADRIAN ISELIN, JR.	MYLES TIERNEY
EUGENE KELLY	VINCENT P. TRAVERS

COMMITTEE ON PRESS AND PRINTING

JAMES M. TULLY, *Chairman*

LOUIS C. BENZIGER	JOSEPH A. KERNAN
EDMUND J. BUTLER	JAMES LEE, M.D.
JAMES S. COLEMAN	JAMES A. MOONEY
THOMAS J. COLTON	BARTHOLOMEW MOYNAHAN
HUGH G. CONNELL	THOMAS MORRISSEY
ANDREW J. CONNICK	VALENTINE MAICKEL
DANIEL F. COHALAN	JOHN W. O'BRIEN
EUGENE P. CLARK	LOUIS V. O'DONOHUE
JOHN J. DELANY	HENRY RIDDER
EDWARD FEENEY	JOHN J. ROONEY
HENRY J. HEIDENIS	HENRY J. SAYERS
CHARLES G. HERBERMANN	WILLIAM F. SHEEHAN
FRANCIS D. HOYT	EDWARD C. SHEEHY
WILLIAM H. HURST	MICHAEL J. SCANLAN
JOHN A. HENNEBERRY	THOMAS F. WOODLOCK

COMMITTEE ON HALL, DECORATIONS AND MUSIC

ANDREW A. McCORMICK, *Chairman*

JOHN ASPELL, M.D.
JAMES BYRNE
THOMAS F. BYRNE
HENRY A. BRANN
CORNELIUS CALLANAN
VICTOR J. DOWLING
PATRICK H. DUNNE
MICHAEL H. DONOVAN
THOMAS GILLERAN
J. HENRY HAGGERTY
PAUL T. KAMMERER
BRYAN L. KENNELLY
ADRIAN T. KIERNAN
JEREMIAH C. LYONS
EDWARD E. McCALL

JOSEPH F. McCOY
JOSEPH J. MEEHAN
THADDEUS MORIARTY
THOMAS MOSHER
ROBERT McGINNIS
OSWALD MAUNE
EDWARD J. McGUIRE
BERNARD NAUGHTON
MILES M. O'BRIEN
DANIEL J. O'CONOR
JOHN J. O'NEILL
P. TECUMSEH SHERMAN
JAMES P. SILO
JOHN B. SEIZ
JOHN TRUNK

COMMITTEE ON RECEPTION

FRANK W. SMITH, *Chairman*

ALFRED V. AMY
EUGENE L. BARNARD
NICHOLAS J. BARRETT
JAMES J. BURKE
WILLIAM J. BOWE
JOSEPH T. BRADY
EDWARD S. CONNELL
JOHN D. CRIMMINS, JR.
W. BOURKE COCKRAN
JOHN J. DEERY
JOSEPH H. FARGIS
JOSEPH P. GRACE
FRANK S. GANNON, JR.
FORBES J. HENNESSY
EDWARD V. HOLLAND

PERCY J. KING
JOSEPH H. McGUIRE
CLARENCE H. MACKEY
JOHN MONKS, JR.
TIMOTHY J. M. MURRAY
GEORGE R. MURPHY
TIMOTHY A. McCARTHY
HAROLD H. O'CONNOR
JOSEPH T. RYAN
H. SCHIEFFELIN SAYERS
WILLIAM J. SWALM
LOUIS M. THIERY
ALFRED J. TALLEY
MYLES TIERNEY, JR.
V. PAUL TRAVERS

The meeting revealed the deep love possessed by the people for their prelate. Long before the appointed hour the great auditorium was packed from floor to dome, and to hundreds of people admission had to be refused. The boxes were filled with representatives of the Catholic society of New York, the chairs crowded to overflowing with delegates from the various societies. The platform was occupied by specially invited guests, representing every order of our municipal life, officials of the city government, judges of the courts, clergymen, among whom were noticed the authorities of the diocese together with the prominent pastors of the city churches, hundreds of the more notable Catholic citizens of New York, with numbers of non-Catholic gentlemen representing various creeds and charitable organizations who had come to testify by their presence to the esteem in which they held the deceased Archbishop. As it was determined that this meeting should be exclusively the mouthpiece of the Catholic laity, no speeches were made by any of the clergy. The Right Rev. Administrator, Bishop Farley, supported by the Right Rev. Mgr. Mooney, V. G., and the Right Rev. Mgr. Edwards, was seated at the side of the presiding officer, Mr. Eugene A. Philbin, a devoted personal friend of the Archbishop. Despite the sorrow that marked the speeches, there was evident a note of exultation at the splendid character of the man whose memory they were praising, and at the greatness of his achievements. For the first time in public were the laymen who loved him so sincerely and so deeply able to say what their hearts dictated, because at other times his presence and his indefinable modesty checked the utterance of what it was felt would be distasteful. The plaintive chant of the surpliced choir of the Paulist Church and the robust magnificent chorals of the united German Catholic societies added deep pathos to an occasion whose sombre character was relieved by the dominant feeling that the memory of a saintly priest, gone to his everlasting reward, was being celebrated. The immense audience waited until the last word had been spoken, and the last note sung, and then dispersed—the spell of reverential awe still hanging over them as they went homewards. The meeting was a magnificent token of the depth of the people's affection for their dead Archbishop, and the words spoken at it deserve preservation. An account of the proceedings is therefore embodied in this memorial.

CARNEGIE HALL

JUNE EIGHTH, NINETEEN HUNDRED AND TWO

Overture—"Marche Funèbre" . . . . DUBOIS
Professor WILLIAM F. PECHER

Chorus—

a—"I know that my Redeemer liveth"
(From "The Messiah," by Handel)

b—"Happy and Blessed are they" . . . . . MENDELSSOHN
CHORUS OF ST. CECILIA
Of the Church of St. Paul the Apostle
Direction of Mr. EDMUND G. HURLEY

Introductory Address . . . Hon. EUGENE A. PHILBIN, *Chairman*

Address . . . . Hon. MORGAN J. O'BRIEN

Address . . . . Hon. THOMAS C. O'SULLIVAN

"Calvary" . . . . RODNEY
CHORUS OF GERMAN CATHOLIC SINGERS
Director, Mr. FRANZ GROSS
Incidental solo parts by Mr. H. HARTMANN, Baritone
Mr. JOSEPH FREY, Tenor
Mr. CHARLES A. O. KORZ, Accompanist

Address . . . . Hon. THOMAS M. MULRY

Address . . . . Hon. JOHN J. DELANY

Address . . . . Hon. CHARLES V. FORNES

Solo—"Ave Maria" . . . . GOUNOD
Miss HILKE
Accompanist, Professor WILLIAM F. PECHER

Address . . . . Hon. W. BOURKE COCKRAN

Chorus—"Nearer, My God, to Thee" . . . . MASON
GERMAN CATHOLIC SINGERS
The audience is requested to join in singing the second verse

HON. LEONARD A. GIEGERICH

Right Reverend Bishop, Reverend Fathers, Ladies and Gentlemen:

I AM instructed by the committee which has arranged for this meeting to announce that it has selected as the presiding officer thereof, Mr. Eugene A. Philbin, whom I now have the pleasure of introducing.

HON. EUGENE A. PHILBIN, CHAIRMAN

Right Reverend Bishop, Reverend Fathers, Ladies and Gentlemen:

WE may well put aside, for the moment, all thought of the great sorrow that fills our hearts, even those who have suffered a real personal loss, and consider rather the virtues and achievements of our beloved Archbishop. It is better to contemplate the characteristics of a great and pious career and to appreciate the lesson it teaches than to utter mere words of sorrow or praise. In this great country of ours, where all men are equal, certainly in opportunity, the personal attributes are the potent factors for good or evil, and, consequently, they are to be judged, and not the position in the community of the individual. Not merely to those who had the privilege of being under his care were the great qualities of the Archbishop known, but even to those outside of his faith. He has been justly described as one of our noblest citizens by a leading newspaper of this city. That such a term was well deserved will be realized when we remember the beneficent influence he exercised over the great majority of those in communion with him. By example and precept he taught those who yielded to his influence that if they would be true Catholics, they must be loyal citizens; that they must perform their duty to their fellow-men, whether the obligation was in private or public life, with no thought of self-interest, but with a sincere appreciation of the opportunity to render service for the betterment of others. Time and time again it has been proved that those who were amenable to his influence derived real inspiration from it, and were faithful to the private or public duty cast upon them, no matter what sacrifice was entailed.

The Archbishop made a most valuable contribution to the cause of good government in the erection and maintenance of the many parochial schools organized during his administration.

Nothing is so essential to the making of good citizens as moral training and education, and where both are combined the best possible results may be expected. The educational system of the Church, by placing the child under the immediate supervision of the pastor, insures attendance at the school and thus obtains not only religious development, but also proper secular education.

His work was unceasing, and while it might well be supposed that such a high office would be surrounded by the luxury and ease of rank, yet it was a fact that his life was most simple, and that he personally gave attention to the merest details of his administration.

He was always accessible to even the humblest of his flock, and ever patient and courteous. The responsibility of his great office never ceased to weigh upon him and to produce the sincere humility so characteristic of men great in intelligent appreciation of opportunity and duty. The Archbishop had a sincere affection for his priests and a genuine interest in all that concerned them. Except in so far as official etiquette demanded, they were truly regarded as co-workers and equals. His great success in the material development of the interests of the Church is eloquent testimony of the splendid and willing coöperation given him by his clergy.

It was his nature to avoid anything like ostentation or honor not made necessary by etiquette or the dignity of his office. He was, as far as circumstances would permit, the same humble priest that I first knew in my boyhood days as Dr. Corrigan, when he was then president of Seton Hall College.

The discipline of the college was perfect, although no harsh words ever passed his lips. He was gentle in manner, but firm in purpose. *Suaviter in modo, fortiter in re.* When the occasion arose for sternness, there was an expression of firmness in his face that at once conveyed the idea that resistance was useless and submission inevitable. He shrank from controversy and contest, but with undaunted courage ever stood ready to uphold the principles it was his duty to support. Gladly would he escape such ordeals so foreign in every way to his true nature, the avoidance of which would often have brought no criticism but the most serious of all consequences to him, the rebuke of his own conscience.

We all know how leniently the world judges an omission of duty and how often it criticizes the performance.

His utter lack of desire to appear in public was well known, and it was only a natural incident of his humility. It was his delight to be with friends to whom he could talk without formality and be on such familiar terms as his natural dignity would permit. Who that enjoyed his friendship cannot readily recall his infectious laugh and his keen appreciation of a good joke? And who when in sorrow has not felt the soothing influence of his heartfelt sympathy? Of his benefactions there is ample testimony in the coffers of every Catholic charity, for there has not been a charitable work of any consequence organized in this city for many years that has not received a substantial contribution from him. And it was not only in money he gave encouragement, but also by his frequent visits to the institutions. On more than one occasion, when I had the privilege of walking with him, we have quietly visited some work of charity, and it was always delightful to observe how sympathetically he would enter into the concerns of the place, and how unaffectedly interested he would be in all its troubles and successes. His last act was to bequeath all his property to the Church.

In short, he loved all mankind and particularly those whom God had given into his care,—his people.

It was not only in the erection of churches and schools that this great love manifested itself, but in his solicitude for the unfortunate in finances or bereavement. No one, no matter how humble, ever appealed to his sympathy in vain, and I know of many instances when despair would have claimed an unhappy victim were it not for his kindly hand.

His great loyalty and devotion to the Church did not preclude a pleasant intercourse with those not of our faith, and never in the history of the Church in this city has there been such a perfect understanding between Catholics and non-

Catholics. Under his administration, bigotry or prejudice practically ceased, and when the Church sought anything it was entitled to it found supporters among those of other faiths. We are to-day working hand in hand with the great Protestant and Hebrew charities, and there is a spirit of brotherly love never before known. The community where all the moral forces are united may hope to attain the ideal of good government. The Archbishop was most strict in his observance of the tenets of the Catholic Church, and felt there could be no compromise as to its teachings and doctrine; but he also felt that mankind could and would be benefited by coöperation in the fields of charity and moral effort. Those who enjoyed the privilege of intimacy with him knew how thoroughly broad he was in Christian charity—what real interest he took in his fellow-man, no matter whether he was of his faith or not.

History will tell of the public works the Archbishop has accomplished. The many structures erected during his administration will remain as monuments of his devotion to the interests of the Church; but of his love for his people, his solicitude for the welfare of the humblest of them, we who have lived under his administration, by assembling here to-night, give testimony to the coming generations.

We may well thank God that it has been given to us to have had our lives influenced by a character so saintly, and by one who stands for all time as a model of a Catholic and a citizen.

THE committee, in arranging the program for to-night, felt that this should be a tribute, purely and simply, by the Catholic laity of New York; and while we knew and appreciated that there were many prominent people not of our faith who would have been glad to add their testimony here, we felt that it should be characteristic of the devotion of his own people to his Grace, and therefore we have confined ourselves to the Catholic laity so far as addresses are concerned.

I regret very much to announce that owing to illness the Hon. Morgan J. O'Brien will be unable to appear here to-night. I shall read the letter which he has sent to me, and I want to say that there was none among the friends of the Archbishop who was more valued than Judge O'Brien, and the great affection which the people of this city, irrespective of religion, have for the Judge was shared by the Archbishop, and he was one of his very closest friends.

My dear Mr. Philbin:

I regret more than I can express that an attack of illness, not serious but sufficient to compel me to remain at home, will prevent my being present at the Memorial Services this evening which are intended to honor the name and perpetuate the memory of our late loved Archbishop. No one could have greater respect for his virtues and talents and his friendship than I. Brought into frequent and intimate personal contact with him, I grew to know and love the man and to revere in him the scholar and the saint. He was not only a sincere friend, a good priest, and an able prelate, but, viewing his character and achievements as a whole, he must ever be regarded as a great man,—great in his fidelity to duty, great in the sincerity and firmness of his convictions, and great because of what he has accomplished. Never have I known a man who was so unsparing of his own comfort and pleasure, and who in the higher planes of human endeavor or in his divine calling, whether in the cause of humanity or religion, so usefully employed every moment of his time and every faculty of his nature, mental and physical. With such sentiments of respect, friendship, and esteem which I have entertained for him, it is a great disappointment that I am unable to-night to publicly pay my simple tribute to his character and memory. Fortunately, however, he needs no commendation of mine, for he lived to see his life filled with honor, deservedly won, and he died lamented by an entire population, irrespective of creed, and will be ever held in fond remembrance of all those who esteemed the true, the beautiful, and the good in the lives of others.

He has fought the good fight, and won, for he has left on earth a priceless heritage of good deeds and noble achievements, and has obtained from Heaven immortality of existence, an eternal crown; and in his life he has proved that blessed is the memory of the just. And though our hearts and prayers will follow him, we have a deep and abiding faith that he will ever rest in peace.

There was no phase of our great Catholicity that the Archbishop took a greater interest in than the work for the young men; and he lived to see the work that had been planned by men who were young in his day carried into successful execution. It is therefore most appropriate that the next speaker has been appointed to address you upon this subject, for he has devoted untiring interest to the welfare of Catholic young men. I have, therefore, the privilege of presenting to you the Hon. Thomas C. O'Sullivan.

HON. THOMAS C. O'SULLIVAN

Mr. Chairman, Right Reverend Bishop, Reverend Fathers, Ladies and Gentlemen:

To BE permitted to voice the sentiments of an assemblage such as this may well be the honor of a lifetime; but to speak of him, the anointed of God, the saintly prelate, the fatherly shepherd now departed from his fold; to speak of him whose voice shall sound in our sanctuaries no more, whose hand, so often lifted in benediction above us, is stilled in death; in this presence to speak of him as he is and shall be enshrined in your hearts and remembered in your prayers forever, is far beyond the reach of any thought or expression of mine. The only qualifications which I bring to the honorable task is the pride of a Catholic New Yorker in the career of his Grace Archbishop Corrigan, and the veneration, love, and sorrow shared with millions of our fellow-citizens for him.

A short time since the eyes of Christendom turned again with wonder and admiration toward the Vicar of Christ in the place of Peter. The ninety-third year of his existence and the twenty-fifth of his pontificate had come to find him still strong in the service of his Master, and countless millions of faithful souls, from the rising to the setting of the sun, were praying, "Long live Leo XIII. May length of years be added to his reign and strength to the hand at the helm of Peter's bark." The American hierarchy, in their greeting to the Holy Father on that occasion, said, "It is well that sons should commemo-

rate a father's glorious and illustrious deeds, which have added
with the flight of years new splendor to the Church of God."
So it is fitting that we, in this metropolis of the Church in the
West, should do honor to the memory of that Christian chieftain whose life amongst us was given to the completion of the
labors handed down to him from his illustrious predecessors.
Theirs was the work of rough-hewing the rock; his the task of
adorning it. Theirs it was to break the soil and protect the
springing fields from the storms that assailed them. His was
the gathering of the harvest and the storing of it for the happiness of all. The requirements of the different epochs in
which they lived demanded men of the stanchest character, but
men of different attainments.

Our country has never known, and not in all the time to come
can it know, better, braver, truer men than those of that generation just gone before us. Of it but a venerable few remain;
the others sleep in the bosom of a land where they won the right
to rest in honored graves. In their youth legions of them came
to this land filled with promise for them, and, wherever toil invited, there they found the way; and wherever they went the
church with the cross was reared, and beside it the humble
school. When clouds of opposition darkened their horizon,
manfully they stood for the faith that was in them; when our
Union tottered in the havoc of war their names were written
on the scroll of American glory. To that generation belonged
the patriot prelate, the giant of the American hierarchy, Archbishop Hughes. Defending the faith wherever attacked, answering his country whenever called, and leading his flock to
fruitful heights, he left to his successors a task which none but
strong men, men of apostolic zeal, could hope to accomplish.
But the gentle, the modest, the unassuming prelate, champion
of the faith, defender of justice and order and lover of his coun-

try, Archbishop Corrigan, responded to every requirement of his high calling in a manner worthy of the great prelates who preceded him.

That the sacred mission intrusted to him was carried to completion countless proofs proclaim. It is attested where suffering and misfortune find solace. It is known where the hand of religion leads the prattling child or closes the eyes of age in their long, last sleep. It is proclaimed by the stately institutions of learning, rising where the humble schools of our fathers stood—the cross-crowned spires looking out into the arches of the American sky proclaim it.

In the days of our beloved Archbishop the American Church had passed the period when her missionary services were due to her children alone. He held that the time had come for society at large to learn her saving truths; he maintained that civil government based upon principles which find their origin in the Church may look to her with confidence as the conservator of justice and order; but beyond all this, inspired with the love of truth and native land, he believed that his countrymen had a right to know the salutary teachings of the Church which he served, and forth amongst them, throughout the land, zealous men of God, encouraged by his support and counsel, went revealing to their countrymen not of the faith the sublime truths of the old Church before the altars of which in a day long gone their ancestors bowed in prayer with yours and mine. And to-night, within the Church and without, wherever there is love for truth and honor for patriotism, there is sorrow for the fatherly shepherd now resting from labor in the peace of God. Though on earth his hand shall never again be raised in benediction above us, we know that from his place on high his blessings shall fall on the land which he loved and the faith which he served.

THE CHAIRMAN

In the great field of charity the Archbishop lived to see a thoroughly organized system developed to the highest possibility in the development of the St. Vincent de Paul Society, and we could have no one more fittingly represent that splendid organization than the speaker whom I now shall introduce, the Hon. Thomas M. Mulry.

HON. THOMAS M. MULRY

Mr. Chairman, Right Reverend Bishop, Reverend Fathers, Ladies and Gentlemen:

To-night for the first time I find myself wishing that I were an eloquent man; for if ever there was a time when one would wish to be blessed with the eloquence of an O'Connell, it is on this occasion, for it would require burning words to picture in their true light the character, the lovable qualities, and the unbounded charity of our sainted Archbishop.

In the few minutes given to me I wish to speak particularly of his love of the poor, and the deep, practical, and earnest interest he took in every good work.

The magnificent qualities which have made his name one of the greatest in the hierarchy of the Church in this country have been and will be most eloquently dilated upon by others to-night. The few plain words which I have to say deal with that quiet inner life, that life which is a distinguishing mark of every true man of God; and those who have had the privilege of association with him in this field know full well that no labor was too great which meant the alleviation of some misery, the lifting up of some fellow-mortal.

To-night brings very forcibly to my mind a notable event, an era, so to speak, in the history of Catholic charity. Four years ago, on this very platform, his Grace the Most Reverend Archbishop addressed an audience made up of representatives of all the charitable societies of the country. It was the opening night of the National Conference of Charities and Correction for the year 1898. It was the first time the Archbishop had ever consented to appear before such an audience, and, made up as it was of people of every shade of opinion in religious and charitable matters, much depended upon the words he spoke. Catholics had every reason to be proud of their Archbishop on that great occasion. The dignity and kindness of his manner, the earnestness of his words, and the spirit of charity which breathed through it all, did more to overcome the prejudices and misunderstandings which had always stood in the way of earnest coöperation than any other means that could have been devised. The effect of his address was felt over the entire country, and his words were quoted as texts for all charity workers, so deeply did they impress themselves upon his hearers.

It would take too long to enumerate a tithe of the great things accomplished by him in this field. The asylums, homes, and societies established and conducted, largely under his control, all with his active encouragement, make a lasting monument to his memory and will ever keep him before us as a truly good shepherd, one who neglected none of his flock.

There never was a man more easy of approach. He was ''at home'' to every one. As a member of the Society of St. Vincent de Paul, it was my great pleasure to be thrown into frequent contact with our dear Archbishop. No one could meet him often without conceiving for him the greatest admiration, and so gracious was his manner that deep affection necessarily followed admiration. It seems hard to realize that he will be no longer with us.

His help was a tower of strength to every good cause. With it there was no fear of failure. His motto was: "What should be done can be done." I remember a beautiful incident in his life which brought out very strongly his great love of the poor. A feeble old woman was climbing up the stairs of the elevated road with a very heavy bundle. His Grace took it from her and carried it to the top. A simple act, but it showed the nobility of his character.

He was continually overrun, as are most men in his position, with begging letters. His custom was to refer such letters to the Society of St. Vincent de Paul, with instructions to help the applicants, if worthy, and send the bill to him.

I never heard him speak an unkind word of any one, and frequently have seen a look of uneasiness in his face when others in his presence spoke uncharitably of absent ones. An editorial in the "Christian Advocate" says of him: "He exerted his power chiefly through personal influence and not by authority, and could not only forgive but forget personal insults."

One of the greatest works the Archbishop accomplished was the development of movements among the laity in the field of charity. The last few years have witnessed a wonderful progress on those lines. We have, to-day, Catholic ladies busily engaged in settlement work, in the care of cancer patients, in rescuing infants and mothers, and as auxiliary committees to hospitals, etc. We have Catholic men engaged in the work of organizing boys' clubs, placing out of children, visiting the poor, and doing other works of charity. Never was the outlook for good works more promising, and certainly this is largely due to the fact that we have been blessed with an archbishop who was, in every true sense of the word, a man of God.

The history of his episcopacy is a grand one, and will be an incentive to those who come after him.

The Society of St. Vincent de Paul has an especial reason for honoring the memory of our sainted Archbishop. He attended the meetings on every occasion possible, encouraged every work in which it was engaged, keeping himself in close touch with all its doings, and was so intimate in his relations with its members that he was looked upon as a brother member. He will be with us no more, but his memory will remain, and our hearts will ever swell with pride and affection when the name of our dear departed Archbishop is mentioned. To-day every member of the Society feels that his loss is a personal loss, a loss which we will long feel and which will take a long time for us to recover from; but his memory, the fragrance of his good and holy life, will incite us to greater efforts and make us try to follow in the footsteps of him who was one of the greatest archbishops New York has ever seen.

THE CHAIRMAN

I HAVE already referred to the Archbishop's devotion to the young man, and I will now ask you to listen to one who has been more active than any other Catholic in organizing the fraternal societies, not only in this great city but throughout the United States, the Hon. John J. Delany.

HON. JOHN J. DELANY

Mr. Chairman, Right Reverend Bishop, Reverend Fathers, Ladies and Gentlemen:

On behalf of the fraternal societies, I venture to pay a tribute of reverence and love to the memory of our departed Archbishop, and to attempt the faint expression of a grief unspeakable. I would not proceed on this occasion beyond this brief utterance were it not that I feel that such a course would do injustice to the living and might seem like dishonor to the dead. It is but just to ourselves that we should acknowledge before all men the loss which we bear, and but honorable that we should avow the gratitude which we cherish toward him who has left us.

In moments of great grief the human heart yearns to give expression to its woe, and what law of matter or of mind can keep back the tears or suppress the anguish of children as they stand around the bier of a well-beloved father?

The intensity of this sorrow impels us to the contemplation of the greatness of his character, and through the tear-drops of our overladen spirit there arises a vision of that extraordinary personality now crowned with the chaplet of immortality. At this solemn moment, with the eyes of the flesh made clear, we realize how great was the man and how great his career. .

In filial pride, with almost choking sobs, we yield to the desire to tell the story of his life and to indulge in reflections upon its meritorious living.

He was born at a time when bigotry against his religion swayed even some of the most benevolent minds, but his death

brought forth expressions of sorrow from hosts of men of
every creed, and was accompanied by a show of toleration be-
tokening a change of feeling to the formation of which his own
public and private life contributed no small share. He was essentially a product of the Church, and men recognized the God-
like strain in the mother who could nurture so God-like a son.
The mark of her sanctity was manifested in the light thrown
upon her by this illustrious offspring.

But those outside the Church who stood afar off beheld only
a meagre manifestation of his high virtues. These were revealed in their fullness to those who confessed with him "one
faith, one hope, one baptism."

He spent his life for his people, and, dying, left them the heritage of his memory. Like Samuel, he served the Lord in the
temple from his childhood, and thus early learned to hearken
to his Master's voice. And thereafter the call never came to
him, whether for labor or for danger, that his soul did not leap
in eagerness to respond, "Lord, here I am." Like a true Levite,
he joined the side of the Lord, and passed from grade to grade
until he reached the priesthood, only to find that the direct care
of souls was to be denied his zealous heart, for his talents
marked him for the task of preparing others for that mission.
But his life-work was not there. He had been but a short time
a professor when he was elevated to the presidency of his diocesan seminary, then made a vicar-general, then administrator of the diocese, and at an age when few men have yet
disclosed the promise of their manhood or are intrusted with
any responsible office in life he was elevated to the government
of one of the great dioceses of the Church.

Merely a student, without training in the stewardship of
finance or the charge of a congregation, he became a bishop—

a leader in Israel. Moses had learned the wisdom of the world in the schools of Egypt, whereas this man's life had been spent in the contemplative cloister. But the oil of the unction, which poured down upon the beard and fell upon the vesture of Aaron, saturated the entire nature of this High Priest, and he received from Heaven, to supply his inexperience, an unerring intuition which all the learning of the world cannot give.

Rapidly passed his remarkably successful seven years' administration of the diocese of Newark. But the boyishness had hardly vanished from his face, at a time of life when holy men tell us the spiritual nature has to meet its worst assaults and the virtue of perseverance its greatest test, when the Holy See appointed him for succession to the Metropolitan of no doubt the largest and most important subordinate see in Christendom.

This is no man's testimony. It is God's. This priest was indeed another Christ.

It was then he came to us. He lived among us and died among us, and we assemble to-night to mingle our gratitude for his life with our lamentations for his death. We owe this duty to a father—it is one of the consolations of paternity—and we offer our homage to his memory for the strong, upright, provident spirit which he displayed in our behalf. But we offer him more than this. Hidden away in the very holy of holies of the heart of every true man there is a sweetly refined love—the love for his mother. It is unlike any other human love. It is born of her unconscious devotion and solicitude and tenderness for her child. It wells up within us as we think of him to-night. Did he not watch over us with a mother's care? Well may we say that "in him was the heart of a woman combined with a heroic spirit and governing mind." Oh! we speak of him with reverence for a father's worth, and offer to his shade a sentiment akin to that which softens us at thought of a dear, dead mother.

I shall not review his work in our midst. A sage has said that that country is indeed a happy one which has no history—whose kings have won no magnificent victories, whose banners have never gone down in defeat. Such is our story,—simply one of progress, and, marvellous though it be, as quiet and benign as the operation of natural law.

And his life was like his administration—one of ceaseless activity, shunning notoriety, suppressing anxiety, dutiful, brave, and discreet. A judge of stainless life himself, he met the erring with a broader charity and a greater benignity than any sinner converted into a saint. A great churchly monarch, he walked our streets with a humility of demeanor which his lowliest subject could not imitate. And his kindliness—oh, how the romping children returning from school, rushing into their homes and breaking the silence, would announce with gleeful voices and sunny faces that they had met the Archbishop on his daily walk and had basked in his smile. And well might they be joyful, for that smile was a veritable benediction.

But on such recollections it is perhaps better that we should not linger. Let us divide, as his children should, the inheritance he has left us. I do not mean the bricks and mortar, the stately churches, the magnificent schools, the hospitals, the orphanages, and the rest. These are material things. The waters may rise and engulf them, the lightning may shatter them, or perhaps the time may come when a godless age shall raze them to the ground. I speak of his enduring heritage to us—the memory of his life.

Of all of us, whose share of this dear inheritance shall be greatest? Oh, marvellous providence! We share alike, bishops, priests, and people, and each of us shall have it all. But has it not been entailed? Has our posterity been forgotten? Oh, wonderful patrimony! We each can eat of it, we each can drink of it, we each can satiate every appetite with it, and it shall not be exhausted, but shall increase from generation unto generation to be a sustenance to our children and their heirs forever.

Why have I spoken of him as if he were dead? Oh, pardon me; they were the thoughts and words of the worldling that escaped me. He is not dead. Such men never die. He lives in our hearts and will live in the hearts of millions. Bishops not yet born shall live his life over by the practice of his virtues; priests shall be ennobled by the contemplation of his example; and the people for whom he strove so hard, for the Christian education of whose children his heart burned out, have learned from him loyalty to the Holy See, and they shall perpetuate his spiritual sovereignty by transmitting to their posterity the saving message his life so well spoke,—to turn their eyes ever for guidance to Peter, for where Peter is there is the Church.

To tell all these things is but to tell how this Christlike man went about his Father's business. For he did his duty to us for Christ's cause, and the glory was all for God. The pebble which the child casts into the sea sets concentric waves in motion, and the force thus liberated shall never cease—its energy shall continue until the material world shall have passed away, but the influence of this holy life shall outlast the annihilation of the universe and shall go on for all eternity.

Oh, what a stupendous miracle is this, that God, so glorified in him living, is even more glorified in him dead!

Alas! his feet do not tread the paths of men, but we are not disconsolate, for the promised reward is his. A crown has in very truth been placed in his mitre, and as we lift up our hearts to the realms where the blessed dwell, and attest our undying love for him and our unflagging devotion to Holy Church, our exalted spirits seem to comprehend a broader and a deeper meaning in the Psalmist's words, and in testimony of him we cry out exultingly before angels and before men: "The Lord hath sworn and it will not repent Him, thou art a priest forever."

THE CHAIRMAN

THERE is a body in this city that represents not only the Catholic sentiment of this great metropolis, but also represents the Catholic sentiment throughout the United States. And within its walls the greatest Catholic movements have been instituted. We have here to-night one who has been president of the Catholic Club for many terms, the Hon. Charles V. Fornes.

HON. CHARLES V. FORNES

Mr. Chairman, Right Reverend Bishop, Reverend Fathers, Ladies and Gentlemen:

THE words which have been so eloquently spoken here to-night and which have touched your hearts and quickened your memory will ever be cherished in sweet recollection of this most memorable yet very sad evening.

The chairman has properly alluded to our late deeply mourned Archbishop as being the father and, so to say, the greatest friend of all institutions, be they the asylums, be they the schools, be they the charities, for which his great heart was so well fitted, or be they the embodiment of the higher aspirations of the mind, the social or the literary life.

That life which he spent in all the noble works which keep men's memories ever green, that life which he devoted to the benefit of the suffering, for the alleviation of pain, that life at the same time was devoted to the highest efforts for the social home of great literary minds. It is, therefore, my great honor, and a memorable event of my life, to briefly allude to the great work which he, in conjunction with those who have stood faithfully by him, did in this direction.

The life of our late illustrious Archbishop during his early days has been referred to eloquently by the preceding speakers, and time being limited, I deem it most appropriate to briefly refer to my pleasant and close business relations with the lamented Archbishop, especially during the erection of the Catholic Club, and by so doing I hope to clearly illustrate the great interest his Grace ever manifested in the literary and social life of his flock and of the community. As the then president of the club, the pleasing duty devolved upon me to acquaint his Grace of the intention of the members to erect a building suitable for the club's constantly increasing library, also to correspond in its appointments with the taste and standard of Catholic social life, and, to more fully insure the success of the work, I called to express the club's desire for his valuable coöperation and friendly encouragement. He listened so intently as to at once assure me of the entire success of my mission. I shall never forget the radiance of his countenance as he spoke, in his memorable gentle tones, of his cordial approval of the club's enterprise, and of his continued interest in its behalf. Gently he rested his hand on my arm, saying, "Yes, it is time that the social work of the Church should be represented by a central home of art, literature, and science." His constant, loving, and generous interest in the welfare of the club is too well known, not only to you here assembled, but throughout the Christian world, to need description here. To show the club to his friends and notable visitors seemed to afford him the greatest pleasure, and those institutions which caused him pleasure should be and are the monuments endearing the memories of his life and worth to present and future generations.

To prove therefore our love and veneration for our late Archbishop, we must sacredly guard and foster the welfare of those institutions which his prayers blessed, and which exemplify his solicitude in any work for sweet charity's sake and for the benefit of mankind.

Scenes of life's experience are living pictures. Therefore scenes wherein we behold the kindly motive, the loving interest, the constancy of purpose, the resolute will, the fearless effort, the consciousness of being right in good deeds for man, the clear conception of duty in harmony with the will of God, made our frequent association with the deceased, endowed with those noble attributes, the source of the most tender remembrance. He was a most worthy and faithful teacher during life's career, the tried, the true friend, in hours of joy and of sorrow, of failures, of success, indeed the priceless companion of life. It surely were desirable to retain with us so noble a character, but the immutable law of nature invites death. The truer the friend the greater the affection; the more noble and numerous the deeds of the departed, the more heartfelt the grief, the more lingering the sorrow, the more irreparable the loss. If this is true, and who dare deny it, then how feeble the language that essays to portray our sense of bereavement at his depar-

ture from us! The silent, restless force ever moving onward to
material success, courageously overcoming obstacles, because
inspired by desire for the weal of man, with the approbation
of God and the hope of reward hereafter, is stilled forever and
must remain with us only as a memory.

Well we may allude to him as our valued friend, whose love
for and interest in us ever prompted kindly thoughts, loyal
words, considerate acts in our behalf. The ring of friendship
was in the sound of his voice. Death came unexpectedly and
rudely awakened the community, the world; its knell in solemn,
sad tones near midnight's hour announced to a flock that loved
him, because he was worthy of their love, that in the prime of
life God had called His servant, who had given the measure of
labor in the field of the Lord. But Death has not conquered
—for it has not dried the spring of love, nor weakened the pulse
of our hearts, nor lessened the ardor of our prayers in his behalf, nor will it diminish the sweetness of memory or eliminate
his deeds for the benefit of religion, charity, education, and our
beloved country. Suffice it to say that the life of the late Most
Reverend Archbishop will become more and more resplendent
as age ripens the fruit in the vineyard of the Lord, wherein
with Christian fortitude he ever labored for the spiritual welfare of man.

THE CHAIRMAN

It hardly needs any words of mine to introduce to you the
gentleman who is now to address you. I will only say that
among the friends of the Archbishop there was none that he
valued more highly or for whom he had a more sincere regard
than the Hon. W. Bourke Cockran.

HON. W. BOURKE COCKRAN

Mr. Chairman, Right Reverend Bishop, Reverend Fathers, Ladies and Gentlemen:

SELDOM in the history of a civilized community has there been paid a tribute so impressive to the success of a prelate, to the zeal of a priest, to the piety of a Catholic, to the virtues of a citizen, to the exceeding gentleness of a gentleman. It is highly creditable to our citizenship that in this tribute men of every creed have participated; that many who rejected the spiritual authority of Archbishop Corrigan are here this evening testifying to their regard for his personal virtues.

The chairman in stating the object of the meeting remarked with his usual lucidity and force that the mere incumbency of this metropolitan see by Archbishop Corrigan is insufficient to explain such a wide-spread demonstration of grief, and I agree with him. Possession of a great office to a capable and devoted man furnishes an opportunity for the display of great qualities; while an incumbent who lacks capacity or devotion merely makes conspicuous defects which in a humbler station would have passed unnoticed, and thus he escapes obscurity only to suffer discredit. We have but to reflect on the vast field occupied and cultivated by the organization of the Catholic Church in this archdiocese—the forces which are actively engaged in executing her beneficent and benevolent purposes, the enterprises of piety, charity, and education which she maintains in constant operation, to appreciate the tremendous task imposed on Archbishop Corrigan by the great office which he filled, and we have but to survey the results of his administration to realize the triumphant success with which that task was discharged.

As we survey what Archbishop Corrigan has accomplished, as we behold the growth of eleemosynary institutions and the multiplication of churches, as we count the schools that have been erected and the number that have been maintained during his administration, we behold a marvellous record of glorious achievements.   Indeed, when I was invited to participate in these exercises I thought my most effective contribution would be a description of the various enterprises which Archbishop Corrigan had undertaken, which he had administered, and which he had carried to completion.   But that idea was soon abandoned, because to give even the most superficial account of them would take more than one hour, and more than one night. In the whole field of human wants and suffering it is impossible to find a difficulty with which he did not grapple or a moral necessity which he did not seek to supply.   Nowhere has suffering wrung the human heart, nowhere has doubt threatened the foundations of belief, nowhere has temptation dogged the footsteps of youth, that he does not seem to have established some institution of piety or charity which remains a light of hope, a fountain of consolation, an outpost of morality, as well as a monument to his efficiency.

The immigrant arriving at our shores, ignorant of our language and our customs, is greeted now by a welcoming friend, eager to give his first steps upon this soil that direction to industry and thrift which often decides the whole character of his life.   Wherever frailty has fallen before temptation, there generous forms are bending to lift it from abasement.   Wherever indigence is unable to provide youth with a proper preparation for life, there pious volunteers supply the training and develop the skill that command ready employment and high wages. Wherever children have been bereft of their natural protectors, there holy women are supplying for the love of Christ the natural affection of which these orphans have been bereft. Wherever adolescence appears to have missed its path and to be drifting toward idleness, vice, and the prison, there a hand is stretched out to reclaim, to educate, to make useful citizens of those in imminent peril of becoming additions to the criminal classes; and the record of the Catholic Protectory is, I believe, unparalleled for its success in reforming youth. In accomplishing these beneficent purposes to which he devoted all his life he necessarily acquired extensive lands, but not one acre could be called his own. He erected stately buildings, yet in not one could he dispose of a single room. He administered vast undertakings, involving great financial risk, yet he left behind him barely sufficient money to cover his funeral expenses. His sole estate is that which was described so eloquently by the gentleman who preceded me, an estate which we are administering here to-night,—of which we are the heirs and the inheritors,—an estate which consists of noble works to which we all join in paying the tribute of our praise, and a memory for saintliness and patriotism to which none refuses the tribute of a tear.

When we consider the talents, the industry, the judgment, the business ability which this man displayed in carrying to success all these varied enterprises of religion and charity, can anybody doubt that if he had exercised the same qualities to gain wealth for himself he would have died among the very richest men in this community? Yet, what estate real or personal that he could have amassed would have so endeared him to his fellows as to have provoked the profound grief with which they learned of his death, and which even this vast meeting is inadequate to express? It is true that if he had used his talents to acquire an enormous fortune he might have bequeathed it to charity or he might have spent his declining days in distributing among educational institutions the money which he had devoted his active years to accumulating, and so his life might have been fruitful of some general benefit. But accepting as his monument all the agencies for good established, maintained, or improved through his zeal—now active in every field of human existence—and which seem to be supplying almost every deficiency in organized society—contrasting their beneficent fruits with the fruits of institutions founded upon bequests or donations of money, however extensive, I believe I am justified in saying that the most valuable gift which man can make to his fellows is the gift of himself, and that was the gift of Archbishop Corrigan.

Of course these vast agencies were almost without exception administered by members of his clergy, but no clergy, however devoted and enthusiastic, can be efficient unless they are efficiently directed by their Bishop. ˙While, therefore, the wealth of this diocese in ecclesiastical, educational, and philanthropic institutions shows that the clergy are zealous, loyal, and efficient in an extraordinary degree, they are also shining monuments to the devotion and the capacity of the Archbishop who so guided and directed his faithful priests that their energies bore the conspicuous fruits which we see on all sides. This efficiency in leadership would have been wholly impossible if he had not himself been the very embodiment of the priestly spirit,—of that priestly spirit which you and I can admire, but which none save those anointed can wholly appreciate or understand. His eulogy as a priest was pronounced on the

day of his funeral by the greatest of pulpit orators. What he
has done for the clergy whom he led and for the religious
orders of which he was the head, the devotion that he displayed to the people whom he lived only to serve, the credit
which he reflected upon the prelacy which he adorned, were described in words almost inspired while his mortal remains lay
before the altar of his Cathedral. And on next Tuesday another illustrious prelate, grown gray in the service of the
Church,—but the growth of whose years has been less rapid
than the growth of popular respect for his virtues,—will voice
the sentiment of the bishops and clergy of this province for
the life and services of their late metropolitan. No words of a
layman could add anything to the weight of these tributes.
His fame as a priest and prelate may well be left to the pane-
gyrics of Archbishop Ryan and Bishop McQuaid. But it is
eminently proper that we as laymen and as citizens of this
great metropolis should celebrate this evening the extent to
which our citizenship has been enriched and dignified by the
ecclesiastical career of Archbishop Corrigan.

The splendor of the tribute which his memory has received
shows the respect in which he was held by all classes of citizens,
Catholic and non-Catholic. Some persons will tell us that the
great popularity which the Roman Catholic hierarchy now en-
joys throughout the country, and which Archbishop Corrigan
enjoyed in an eminent degree, is a result of some change or
other in the Catholic Church; that the Catholic Church is not
what she was; that the attitude of the public has changed to
her because she has changed in some respects in her attitude
toward faith or toward morals. No assumption could be more
profoundly mistaken. The Catholic Church is unchanged and
unchangeable, for her foundation is the immutable truth which

she was established to defend. What she was in the beginning of her mission, that she is to-day; and that we have the promise of God she will continue to be until the consummation of the world.

With the progress of civilization the field of a Catholic prelate's activities has changed to some extent, not because the faith committed to his guardianship has changed in the slightest degree, but because the social, economic, and political conditions of men have changed, and these changes are largely the product of Catholic faith, Catholic teaching, and Catholic courage.

It is said, for instance, that the Catholic Church has been hostile to liberty and to republicanism, whereas in truth and in fact Catholicism is the true fountain of rational liberty. It is to Catholicism that republicanism owes its birth. The influence of the one has kept pace with the growth of the other throughout the world; and Catholicism is the only basis upon which republicanism can rest with any security. There is but one argument against republicanism, and it is that if control of government be intrusted to a whole people its powers would be abused, because the masses of men are not sufficiently virtuous to be trusted with control over the lives and property of each other. The mission of the Church from her foundation by our Divine Lord has been the moral improvement of each individual. If Christianity and Catholicism were triumphant throughout the world,—that is to say, if all men, besides professing belief in Catholic doctrine, actually governed their lives by it,—then each man would be pure, each man would be just, each man would be loyal; and with a people composed of such units no government but republicanism would be possible. Catholicism becoming general, republicanism becomes universal.

This is not abstract speculation, but an inevitable deduction from the unquestioned truths of history. Every right which we deem essential to the enjoyment of civil liberty has its origin in Catholic truth, and was first asserted by Catholic prelates for the welfare of their flocks. It is certainly true that at the threshold of modern progress, when the ancient civilization had fallen, and while the barbarians who had overwhelmed it were still swarming over Europe, justice seemed to be without champions, freedom without advocates, and mercy without ministers, except as we can discern through the ruin of war, the confusion of battle, and the smoke of pillage the figures of Catholic missionaries—confessors and prelates—always following close on the heels of invading hosts, laboring to alleviate the horrors of invasion and the rigors of conquest. The savage warriors who held in profound contempt the effeminate and incompetent defenders of the old Empire looked first with interest, then with respect, and finally with awe, upon these intrepid champions who, disdainful of their own safety, watched jealously over the welfare of others, who could not be deterred by flights of arrows or charging squadrons from fields of carnage while there remained a chance to succor a wounded or to shrive a dying man; and through the moral influence established by their piety, courage, and devotion to humanity, Catholic prelates succeeded in securing from the conquerors the first concessions of civil rights which were the foundation of modern civilization and the dawn of modern liberty.

To show the part which Catholic prelates played in establishing civil liberty, I need mention but one man, Stephen Langton, who by combining the English clergy and the English barons in a demand that the laws of the good King Edward be restored, succeeded in wresting Magna Charta from King John. And yet, men who tell us to-day that Catholicism is inconsistent with liberty will at the same time declare that all civil freedom in America and England dates from Magna Charta, itself the fruit of episcopal zeal and patriotism in Great Britain.

Times have changed and improved since Catholic bishops were compelled to face the sword of tyranny that the personal rights of those whom they fed with the bread of life might be saved from savage oppression. Archbishop Corrigan lived in an age when there was no longer occasion for priests to confront kings and bid them pause before they outraged justice; but if during his incumbency of this see an occasion had arisen which made it necessary for him to risk his life in order to save his flock from injury, moral or material, could anybody who knew him doubt that he would have been ready to die upon the steps of his altar like Thomas à Becket; or if a pestilence had ravaged this city and terror of it had driven all others to seek safety in flight, that he, like Charles Borromeo, would have remained in his field of duty, helping the sick, visiting the dying, risking his life ten thousand times rather than let the humblest of his subjects go unshriven into the presence of God?

While the heroic days have passed away when loyalty of Catholic prelates to duty involved peril to their lives, the mission of a bishop is still as important to the state as ever it was. The elementary rights of man are now conceded everywhere, at least throughout Christendom. The right of every man to enjoy the property created by his labor is acknowledged in every civilized state. The peril to liberty is no longer in the tyranny of kings or classes, but in the possible failure of the masses to exercise with wisdom and moderation the extensive powers they have acquired. The most important service ever rendered by the Church to civilization is not behind but before her,—that of preventing the extensive rights now enjoyed by the citizen from being abused to his own injury through ignorance or through immorality. The failure of a government built upon faith in popular virtue would be a calamity of measureless proportions, for by discrediting institutions of freedom it would inevitably provoke a reaction toward autocratic or aristocratic government.

In a republic the Church is the most effective agent for maintaining the security of the state. A monarchy may rest upon coercion, for it does not ask but compels the obedience of its subjects. A republic cannot rest on any other foundation than the consent, support, and voluntary obedience of the majority of its citizens, for where obedience is enforced upon a majority the government is not republican, whatever else may be its form. A republic is impossible unless it is pillared upon virtuous women and loyal men,—loyal not merely in outward conduct, but in heart, in spirit, and in thought. Yet while loyalty in this sense is essential to its very existence, a republic has no means of compelling it. All that a state can do is to coerce. It can prohibit an act or enjoin one under a penalty. It cannot reach the mind or heart of the citizen. The Church alone can reach the springs of human action, for it alone deals directly with the mind and the soul. Everything which the Church does, every duty that she enjoins, every penance that she imposes, every rite that she prescribes, has for its object the moral improvement of the individual, and what improves him morally makes him fitter for citizenship. Obviously the man who attends the Catholic Church, accepts her doctrines, and conforms his life to her precepts, will yield voluntary obedience to law without the intervention of policemen or any form of coercion; and the good Catholic is therefore necessarily the good citizen, the reliable pillar of republican government. Every day of Archbishop Corrigan's sacerdotal life, every hour of his episcopal service was devoted to making men loyal to civic duty by developing and encouraging the virtues which made them fit for communion with the Church, and the success which he achieved made him preëminently the champion of justice and the upholder of order in this metropolis.

In no way did he contribute more effectively to the maintenance of peace and order in this community than by the zeal and fervor with which he maintained the principle of authority. Some people believe that we Catholics, in recognizing the right of the Church to interpret authoritatively the Scriptures, are surrendering some natural freedom of intellect. This misapprehension might be natural in an autocratic government, but it is almost incomprehensible in this republic. The one feature which distinguishes this highly successful government from all the republican experiments that have ended in failure and disaster is the principle of authority which it establishes, by equipping one department with the right to determine authoritatively and finally the limits of power for all other departments in our political system. It is not the Constitution as written by its authors, but the Constitution as interpreted by the courts, that as the supreme organic law of this country has established and maintained the most durable and beneficent government in the whole experience of mankind.

Now, Catholics believe that the bounty of the Lord was not exhausted when he uttered the Word of salvation. We believe His mercy went further,—that he not only revealed to us His Word, but He gave us an infallible means of interpret-

ing it when He established the Church of which Archbishop
Corrigan was the head in this diocese. The moral law which
governs Christians we Catholics believe is not merely the
gospel as it is written, but the gospel as it is interpreted by the
Church.

During the month of April last it was my high privilege to
have an audience with our Holy Father the Pope, in the course
of which, alluding to this very principle of authority, he said
that in this country, above all others, the Church should be
cherished by men of every faith, for she had always maintained
in things spiritual that principle of authority which all Americans believe absolutely essential in civil government. That
authority, however, was not a privilege to be enjoyed by the
Pope who governed her, but a burden of duty imposed on him
by his sacred office. "For," said he, with that impressive manner and in that vibrant voice which lends such weight and
charm to all his utterances, "this authority committed to these
hands—all unworthy though they be—cannot be used for my
benefit or my glory. Every interpretation of the law that I
make is binding upon me as it is upon the humblest of my subjects; authority is given to me only that I may exercise it to
keep open before the footsteps of men the pathway to salvation
marked out for them by our Divine Lord Himself."

My friends, the Archbishop of New York is the deputy of
the Pontiff to keep that pathway open and unobstructed in this
diocese, and never during the incumbency of Michael Augustine Corrigan was any obstacle of false philosophy or of false
theology suffered to encumber it or to obstruct it. As the
depositary of the law he was faithful unto death, but if he was
inexorable in declaring it he was scrupulous in obeying it. He
had the right to dispense in some respects, but his dispensa-

tions were always for others. Rigid, unqualified, unceasing obedience to the law in its every letter he always imposed on himself.

It has been said that he was not a member of what is called the liberal school of thought. Well, he was not,—if by liberalism is meant to observe outwardly the ceremonies of the Catholic Church while inwardly doubting her doctrines. Archbishop Corrigan believed that every word of the Gospel must be true, or else that none of it is true; that it is all the Word of God, or it is the work of God's enemy; that unless it is Revelation it is imposture. He could not understand how any man professing to be a Catholic could doubt a single word of the revelation on which Catholicism rests, or how any man clothed with episcopal powers and charged with episcopal duties could permit a person to remain in outward communion with the Church who rejected any one of her doctrines. The faith was not his, that he could relax it or be liberal with it. He was but the custodian of it. He was not the fountain of it, but the channel through which it flowed to the faithful. As an honest, an honorable, and a truthful man he had, therefore, no course but to insist that implicit acceptance of every word of that sacred revelation was the condition of belonging to the communion of the Catholic Church. A man was a Catholic or he was not. If he was a Catholic he believed. If he did not believe he was not a Catholic. If he was not a Catholic he might be prayed for, but he could not be recognized as one. If he refused to believe in the doctrines of the Church or to comply with her discipline, that refusal placed him outside her communion. If he repented, gladly was he welcomed back. If he did not repent he was pursued by love, by interest, by prayers, never by dislike or rancorous words. No man could be excluded from the Church by anybody but himself. The key to readmission was always in his own hands, but till he conformed and believed he had no fellowship with the Catholic Church.

While Archbishop Corrigan was unswerving in defence of the truth, he never lost his temper in a discussion. I never knew any person so charitable to all who differed with him. He was one of those who believe that there is no excuse or reason for allowing differences on matters of belief or opinion to become grounds of personal quarrel. If a man did not consider his beliefs on any subject the best in the world, he should change them. While he held them, it was evident that he believed them to be the best; and if they were the best, then any contrary opinions must necessarily be inferior. Now, no man quarrels with his neighbor because he has inferior horses, or houses, or clothes, but he may quarrel with him if he has some doubt about their inferiority. So it is with opinions. No man who is quite sure of his own beliefs ever quarrels with a neighbor for differing from him. Ill temper in discussion betrays doubt about the soundness of his own beliefs.

What were the personal qualities by which the wonderful results were achieved, so well described by the distinguished gentleman who preceded me? The fruits of his episcopal career I need not describe. They are visible on every side. Whoever wants to realize them has but to look around him. But those who were personally acquainted with him—above all, those who enjoyed the great privilege of admission to his intimacy—could discern in his virtues, his abilities, his laborious industry, his consideration for all men, and his loyalty to friends, the explanation of his extraordinary success in holding the warm affection of his spiritual subjects and in conquering the unqualified respect of the whole community.

In every relation of life he was gentle, firm, charitable, loyal, courageous, and capable. Upon the altar his piety was conspicuous. When he assumed his pontifical robes and engaged in an episcopal function his bearing was impressive, even majestic. In the pulpit he was convincing and always interesting. You may ask, Was he eloquent? The answer would depend upon how you interpret the word. Once asked to discuss eloquence, I defined it as sincerity, and I have never had any reason to change the definition. The man who never speaks except to convey an idea which he believes will benefit his auditors; who never seeks to display his own capacity in verbal gymnastics, and never uses a word that is not necessary to express his meaning,—that man cannot fail to be impressive, that man cannot fail to be eloquent, because that man is sincere. I know of nothing more remarkable than the instinct of an audience for sincerity on the part of a speaker. It is matter of common remark that elaborately framed sentences and highly polished periods from the lips of one man sometimes fall upon listless or inattentive ears, while another man whose language is wholly unstudied will be listened to with rapt attention; and the explanation is not far to seek. One man is sincere; the other is not. One man speaks for the benefit of his hearers; the other, to exploit himself. Archbishop Corrigan never went into the pulpit unless he was under the spur of a conviction, a principle, a truth, that he felt it his duty to explain for the welfare of the people. He never obtruded his own personality between his audience and the subject under discussion, and the upturned eyes of his hearers showed the hold that he had established upon their hearts and minds. His was not the eloquence that men talk about, but it was the eloquence that men listen to. It was not the eloquence that amuses men, but it was

the eloquence that convinces them. It was not the eloquence
that left persons discussing the phrases that he had used or the
rhetoric that he had employed, but it was the eloquence that
left them discussing or considering the truths that he had ex-
pounded. If this be not eloquence, then he was not eloquent.
But if that be the highest form of eloquence which rivets attention, awakens reflection, and stimulates discussion, then he was
one of the strongest pulpit orators that I have ever heard in
this or any other community.

His learning was remarkable. From his very early youth it
had attracted the attention of his superiors and won for him
the chief prizes of scholastic proficiency, while in later years
it was undoubtedly a decisive element in winning for him rapid
promotion to the archiepiscopal throne. But the subjects
which he loved to study and on which his mind loved to dwell
were not the injuries done by men to each other, but the benefits wrought by men for the human race. He cared little about
wars or conquest. He studied them only that he might understand the causes which had operated to promote civilization
and those which had retarded it. But he loved to read the lives
of the saints. He loved to dwell upon the sacrifices of those
holy men who had spent their lives in renunciation of themselves and in unflagging devotion to others. Following their
example, he never thought of his own interests, but always of
the souls committed to his charge; and because he was never
occupied about himself he became the preoccupation of all his
friends. His learning was not a torrent that bore him into violent controversy, but a placid though majestic tide that carried
others with him to the sound conclusions that he had reached,
and to the lofty purposes animating his own life.

If I were asked to mention his distinguishing characteristic,

I should say it was simplicity; and with men as with machines simplicity is the characteristic of excellence. He was, I think, the shrewdest judge of human nature that I ever knew, yet he was singularly simple and direct in all his mental operations. From my observation and knowledge of him I have come to the conclusion that nobody is so little likely to be deceived as a man who is himself incapable of deception. Indeed, I begin to doubt if any one can be deceived by a lie except a liar. It seems as if the candid are endowed with an instinct for truth which warns them of the approach of mendacity. Archbishop Corrigan did not seem to have the intellectual capacity to digest a falsehood; by instinct rather than by judgment he rejected it immediately. In his ear, attuned to truth and simplicity, an equivocal or doubtful statement rang false, just as a counterfeit coin rings false in the ear of a bank officer accustomed to the sound of honest money; and though he met all men with generous confidence, I don't believe any person ever succeeded in deceiving him.

Toward discussion of his administration, of himself or his conduct, his attitude was that of the broadest charity, and, therefore, of the most perfect philosophy. He regarded criticism not as an injury to be resented, but as a benefit for which every man should be grateful. If it were well founded it revealed a fault and was therefore a step toward its correction; while if unfounded it was a high compliment, because it showed that in order to criticise you one had to invent his grounds of criticism. His critic, therefore, he held was always either a benefactor or a flatterer; under no circumstances would he regard him as an enemy.

I believe he was without a single enmity. I don't believe there was a human being he would not have taken infinite pains to serve, while for a friend he would have sacrificed anything but his episcopal robe. Many people will tell you that unless a man has enemies he cannot have friends, but here was a man who disliked no one, but was capable of the warmest attachments. His friendships were bounded only by the moral law. For a friend he would sacrifice everything he possessed except a conviction of duty, and to that every personal affection, tie, or ambition must be sacrificed. Duty was the animating purpose of his soul and the governing rule of his conduct. Devotion to it was reflected in all his actions and explained all his characteristics. His preëminent quality was his gentleness. Yet, though his hands were infinitely gentle in feeding his flock, they were hands of steel when it became a question of defending the fold. In discussing him with our Holy Father, Leo XIII, that great Pontiff referred to him as "a great prelate and a saintly man." That is the epitaph which, I think, should be inscribed upon his tomb: "A great prelate and a saintly man!" It describes him faithfully, and it exhausts the language of praise for an ecclesiastic. It was the conviction which dominated the vast throngs of men and women who passed through the Cathedral while his remains lay in state; which found expression in the sobs of his spiritual children and in the sighs of his fellow-citizens rising to heaven from around his bier.

I was profoundly impressed by the gentleman who spoke of the estate that Archbishop Corrigan left behind him. Well may he say that this estate is not to be measured by the buildings which he erected nor by the institutions which he administered. Who can measure the influence of a good life? Who can measure the influence of inspiring words that are spoken and noble deeds that are performed in conspicuous station for

the love of God and the love of God's children? Can any man
measure the influence of the light which bathed this earth in
the course of the last year, or even of a single ray of sunshine
escaping from the dark clouds of a winter's day, or of the
winds that last March bent the trees in yonder park, or even of
a single gust which, blowing through some distant farmyard,
may have caught up a single seed, borne it across the sea, and
dropped it on some coral reef, there to become the source of a
gorgeous vegetation of swaying grasses, fragrant flowers, and
stately palms, which ages hence will delight the eyes of countless thousands? Yet it would be easier to measure the influence
of all the sunshine that falls upon this earth in all the years
that this sidereal system has witnessed,—the influence of all the
rivers that have flown to the sea, and of every drop of water
between their banks,—the influence of every breeze that has
blown from the four quarters of the globe, than to measure the
influence—the permanent growing influence—for good of a life
spent in unselfish devotion to God, to humanity, and to country.

No word of admonition that Archbishop Corrigan has
spoken can ever be lost. No deed of piety which he wrought
can be destroyed. They will be effective while time lasts.
Their fruits will be better men and purer women, a broader
conception of citizenship, and keener loyalty to its duties
among all who acknowledged his authority or admired his virtues; and the influence of a generation so inspired will extend
to all the generations that are to follow. Not the towers of the
Cathedral which he completed; not the Seminary which he built
at Yonkers; not the churches which he dedicated; not the asylums which he established; not the schools which he maintained
shall be his monument. Oh, no! The structures of stone in
which he exercised his functions shall all pass away; their very

ruins will perish; but his influence will remain and survive them all. His enduring monument will be this see which he has filled, which he has adorned, which he has made a shining light of progress throughout Christendom—this city which he left the capital of the United States, and which, under the influence of the virtues inculcated by his words and illustrated by his example, is destined to become the capital of civilization throughout the world.

THE MOURNING OF THE LEVITES

THE ARCHBISHOP AND ST. JOSEPH'S SEMINARY, DUNWOODIE

THE first announcement of the serious nature of the Archbishop's illness fell like a pall upon the Seminary at Dunwoodie, when professors and students were alike oppressed with fear and dread of the loss that threatened. Night and morning prayers were offered up in common for his recovery, and every evening before retiring the students sang, with an unction indicative of their affection and anxiety, the "Oremus pro Antistite Nostro."

Only too willing to catch at any ray of hope, they heard with joy on the evening of the 5th the favorable reports given out in regard to the Archbishop's condition. Few, if any, had any forebodings of the sad news of the morrow. It was nearly midnight when the rector was reached by telephone from the Cathedral, and he immediately awakened the professors with the brief, but startling announcement, "Our Archbishop is dead!"

The next morning, at 6.30 o'clock, a Solemn Mass of Requiem was sung in the main chapel of the Seminary for the repose of the soul of the deceased prelate. The Very Rev. E. R. Dyer, rector of the Seminary, was the celebrant. At all the other altars Low Masses were said for the same intention by the professors of the Seminary.

In the evening the Very Rev. Rector addressed the students on the life and character of the Archbishop, his intense fatherly

129

interest in the Seminary, and the influence which his memory should long exert over them.

With as little delay as possible the façade and the chapel were draped in purple and black. The exterior drapery was not removed until the departure of the students for their summer vacation, while that in the chapel was allowed to remain until after the annual retreat of the clergy.

On June 17, two days before the departure of the students, another Solemn Requiem was sung in the Seminary—the Very Rev. Rector again being the celebrant, and Revs. Jas. Fitzsimmons and John R. Mahoney, professors of the Seminary, deacon and subdeacon respectively. The sermon (the full text of which is given in these pages) was preached by Rev. R. K. Wakeham, S.S., also of the Seminary.

Among those present were Rt. Rev. John Edwards, Rt. Rev. J. S. M. Lynch, of Utica, Very Rev. Fr. McKenna, O.P., Rev. George Corrigan and Dr. Joseph Corrigan, brothers of the Archbishop. Besides these nearly one hundred priests assisted, chiefly from the city and archdiocese.

On June 18 the Feast of the Holy Priesthood was celebrated as the usual closing exercise of the Seminary.

The Meditation on the occasion was given by Rev. Joseph Bruneau, S.S., who spoke feelingly and forcibly of the Archbishop as the model priest in his faith, piety, and self-sacrifice.

The following tribute to the Archbishop is taken from the last issue of the Seminary Catalogue:

Archbishop Corrigan

From a portrait in oil by Gagliardi, Rome, 1901

ARCHBISHOP CORRIGAN

IN MEMORIAM

ON the evening of May 5, 1902, the Most Rev. Michael Augustine Corrigan, Archbishop of New York, passed to his reward. His death is a grave loss to the diocese over which he ruled, and to the whole Church in America, but is nowhere more keenly felt than in this institution, of which he was the founder, patron, and guide.

Of the many titles which he possessed to the lasting and grateful remembrance of future generations of American Catholics, probably the most striking was his persistent zeal in the cause of Catholic education. In the matter of priestly education, his zeal for learning and religion was intensified by his great love for his priests, his deep personal interest in their welfare, and his intense desire that they should be worthy of their high calling. None of the many important duties of his exalted position appealed to him more strongly than that of training up a learned, cultured, and pious body of priests to minister to the Catholic people. His plans were matured in the most broad-minded and far-sighted spirit, and were carried into execution with triumphant success by the coöperation of a generous clergy and laity whom he had imbued with his own spirit and zeal. But the most active of his assistants in the work will acknowledge that it is to his clear mind and strong will and unceasing labor that is due the realization of the hopes and dreams of Catholic educators in the building and equipment of a model seminary.

Such was his personal share in every detail of the work that those who knew him best find in the structure and arrangements of the Seminary striking indications of his character. The combination of simplicity and strength which formed his most striking characteristic is evident in the Seminary; his love of thoroughness and attention to detail are shown by the fact that no part of the building, from basement to attic, has been slighted or neglected; his kindness and thoughtfulness · are manifest in the arrangements made for the sick; his broadmindedness, in the opening of the whole library to the students without reserve; his refinement of character, in the encouragement of everything that tends to refine without effeminating; his willingness to accept the best results of modern invention, in his adoption of all the latest methods and improvements; and his intense devotion to religion and strict adherence to its observances, in the construction and equipment of the chapel of the Seminary.

As for his generosity, it is beyond showing or telling. He defrayed from his private fortune the entire cost of the beautiful chapel; he would allow no one to contribute as much as a window or a statue to it; it was to be his own contribution to the work, and it certainly is a worthy one—a monument to his generosity and piety. He considered the library as, after the chapel, a second power-house of the institution. He contributed to it at the beginning the PRESTON and MAGOON collections, and, from his frequent benefactions, it was evidently much in his mind. On the happy occasion when, in presence of two hundred and fifty of his priests, he was able to consecrate the Seminary chapel, he presented a paid-up life insurance policy of $10,000 to endow the library.

His interest in the Seminary was not merely that of a munificent builder or financial patron. It extended to every man within its walls and to every detail of its management. Though he followed in this matter, as in all his dealings with his priests, his wise policy of confidence in the men appointed to a duty, his interest in the affairs of the Seminary was evinced in numerous ways. All matters of importance in the management of the institution were submitted to him, and, though he rarely made modifications in matters on which the faculty had a definite settlement to propose, his quick appreciation, his deep interest, his hearty sympathy with every plan for betterment, made it a pleasure as well as a duty to consult him.

There is a certain sad pleasure in knowing that the Seminary was in his thoughts until the last. On the evening of his death, as his brother was leaving his room, he called him back to ask him to look over the plans for the contemplated addition to the Seminary building. It was indeed appropriate that the active mind and energetic will which had been busied so long in the service of religion should be occupied even to the time of death with plans for further labors and sacrifices in the service of God and humanity to which this institution is dedicated.

He had frequently expressed to those intimate with him his intention that, when the burden of years should come upon him, if it were God's will that he should grow old in His service, he would delegate the more onerous of his duties and would himself retire to his beloved Seminary, there to spend his remaining years in peace and prayer amongst the quiet surroundings of this restful spot. Imagination dwells with pleasure and regret over this unrealized plan. For him it would have brought, after a life of toil and struggle, a measure of that peace and recollection so agreeable to his natural disposition. The directors of the Seminary would have had the strength of his presence, the help of his strong, well-stored mind, his deep knowledge of human nature and of life, his fine Catholic spirit, and the charm of association with this unobtrusive, kindly man of God. The future generation of priests would derive the advantage of knowing, by personal intercourse, the kindness which they can now know only by his deeds of generosity, and of having before their eyes in the venerable priest and prelate a model of study, of prayer, of confidence in God, of humility and simplicity of life and character which no loftiness of position had power to change.

It has been ordered otherwise. He has been called away from us in the height of his power for good. We accept the decree of God with sadness, but with that confidence in His Providence which was the comfort and support of the departed. It is a solace to be able to think that he is receiving, in a measure which no place on earth could give, the only true refreshment, light, and peace; and that by his prayers to the great High Priest in heaven, he can still help us more than he could by his continued presence to acquire the virtues he manifested, and to carry on the work he began for the formation of the Christian priesthood and the upbuilding of the Church of God.

THE SEMINARY A MONUMENT OF THE ARCH-BISHOP'S ZEAL FOR THE GLORY OF THE HOUSE OF GOD

(Sermon by Rev. R. K. Wakeham, S.S., June 17)

I have loved, O Lord, the beauty of Thy house, and the place where Thy glory dwelleth. Ps. xxv: 8.

Rt. Rev., Very Rev., and Rev. Fathers, and Young Gentlemen, Students of St. Joseph's Seminary:

Though six weeks ago to-day our altars were draped and our first Solemn Requiem was offered up for the repose of the soul of our beloved Archbishop—even before the sleeping millions had awakened to be startled and grief-stricken by the announcement of the sad loss that had fallen upon this archdiocese, and upon the whole Church in the United States—nevertheless it is most fitting that once more, on the eve of our closing, we should give expression to our love and our gratitude by offering up the Adorable Sacrifice of Propitiation in behalf of our Father and Benefactor.

It is most fitting, too, Rev. Fathers, that you should have a share in this offering; for, by your presence here to-day, you add to this act of impetration a completeness and an appropriateness than which nothing could, I am sure, be more pleasing or consoling to the heart of our beloved Archbishop.

Our first thought then, to-day, as it is also our first duty, is to beseech God to deal mercifully with His faithful servant,

whose stewardship was so vast, and whose responsibility was proportionally great.

Forty years of priesthood,[1] — even the humblest and least trying position that may fall to the lot of a priest, is, indeed, a terrible responsibility. Thirty years of episcopate, in the smallest diocese and under the most favorable circumstances, is a responsibility incomparably greater—and I need not say why. Who then can form an adequate conception of the account to be rendered for such a stewardship as was intrusted to him during the last fifteen or seventeen years of his life? Who would wish to stand before the tribunal of Eternal Justice and answer for the reckoning?

St. Paul doubtless understood the full extent of this responsibility, and he reminds us of our own share in it when he says to us: "Remember your prelates who have spoken the word of God to you. . . . Obey them and be subject to them. For they watch *as having to render an account of your souls.*" Heb. xliii: 7, 17.

Hence our sacred obligation, not only in charity and in gratitude, but also in strict justice, to offer up the Adorable Sacrifice and our own feeble prayers for one who has borne so great a burden, not for himself alone, but for his fellow-men, and for the honor and glory of God.

But, Rev. Fathers, however appalling this responsibility, however rigorous the account demanded, whatever errors or defects may have been revealed by the search-light of Divine Justice, our Archbishop had, at least, *one grand plea* to enter in his own behalf, one which few other mortals have ever been able to offer with more sincerity, more unfaltering confi-

---

[1] Ordained priest, 1863; consecrated bishop, 1873; became Archbishop of New York, 1885.

dence, when standing before that dread tribunal, the greatest, the most powerful plea that any priest or prelate may ever hope to offer. For I am sure, Rev. Fathers, that there is not one among you that will not affirm (and those among you who have known him longest and most intimately will assert it most emphatically) that you have never known any one who could stand before the Sovereign Judge and say with greater confidence and more absolute truth, '' I have loved, O Lord, the beauty of Thy house, and the place where Thy glory dwelleth.''

You have seen numberless proofs of this in his synodal decrees; in his canonical visits, so regularly made to the parishes of his vast diocese; in his constant solicitude for the erection of magnificent churches and beautiful chapels; in his untiring zeal for the decency, splendor, and ritual accuracy of Divine worship.

But I think it may be said without fear of contradiction or dissent, that the greatest evidence we have of this love of his for the beauty of the house of God, *is here, in this very institution*, which he founded and brought into actual existence,—which he loved as the apple of his eye,—which he regarded as the crowning work of his life,—and which was almost the last subject of his thoughts and interest—save alone the affairs of his own soul, and his relations with God.

What the Archbishop accomplished on the broader lines and in the more public affairs of his arduous and important administration, has been fully and admirably set forth by two of the most eloquent, justly popular and revered members of the American hierarchy, and has received commendation from prominent members of the laity, as well as from the press of the country, regardless of creed or party, religious or political.

An eloquent tribute has also been paid to his unsurpassed and uncompromising zeal for the cause of Catholic, and, especially, of ecclesiastical education.

But, while it is with unfeigned diffidence that I venture to approach the subject, I feel that this is the proper occasion to speak, even at some length, of the real significance and importance of this great work—*the founding and erection of the Seminary*. And though I may fail in part of what I attempt, I hope that I may at least succeed in saying something that may be of lasting benefit to those who are now enjoying the advantages provided for them by his zeal and munificence.

The fame of this institution for its architectural merits, and the excellence (or, as some have supposed, the extravagance) of its material equipment, has gone forth to the uttermost limits of our own country, and even far beyond. As it really stands, it has seldom, if ever, failed to elicit the admiration of those who have seen it; while few have ever obtained a correct or an adequate idea of it from descriptions, however faithfully or enthusiastically given.

But while admitting what many would call its monumental grandeur, there has not been entire unanimity of opinion as to its practical adaptation to the purpose for which it was intended.

Some have looked upon it as, at least, a doubtful experiment. Some as a bold and almost reckless departure from time-honored methods and conditions. Some have even gone so far as to exclaim in the words of one whose own *preparation for the priesthood* proved a woeful failure, "Ut quid perditio haec?"

In all these appreciations there was, it seems to me, one very grave oversight, viz.: that those who were thus passing judgment forgot to ask, " Who is responsible for this new departure? What is his reputation as a man of prudence and experience? Is he known as being fond of the novel and the sensational? Does he strive or manage to keep himself before the public by startling novelties? Or does he belong to the so-called ultra liberal and progressive school? Has he the reputation of making little account of sacred traditions, the decrees of Councils, and the well-known spirit and teachings of the Church? Or is he one who would wish, for the sake of vain display, to raise up a generation of effeminate, flippant, and worldly-minded priests?"

Perhaps if some of these questions had been asked (more seriously and honestly, of course, than Pilate asked, " What is truth?") the suspicion, at least, might have arisen that, after all, there must have been some prudence, and some wisdom, and some zeal for religion behind so great an undertaking, however much it may have the appearance of a new and radical departure.

Be that as it may, we, Rev. Fathers, need not ask any of these questions. But I think it well worth our while,—and the occasion is appropriate,—to examine as far as we may into the Archbishop's own concept of this great work. For I believe that we shall find it to be as broad, as lofty, as comprehensive, and as thoroughly adapted to the attainment of the greatest and best results to be expected from a seminary as any plan that has ever been conceived and carried into execution. I am speaking now merely of the material edifice; but I hope to show that it is, as he intended it should be, a great moral factor in producing the desired results.

In the first place, no one who knew the Archbishop can doubt for a moment that he desired to have in his Seminary *three things* which all consider to be absolutely essential: *solid piety,*

thorough discipline, and an efficient course of clerical studies.
But to these three he wished that a fourth should be added,
viz.: a training in proper ecclesiastical deportment and refinement. These, and all of these, he was determined to have at all
costs. This, however, was far from being all that was comprised in his idea of a seminary. He did not consider that,
even when these results were attained, and attained in the most
perfect manner possible, *the whole mission* of a seminary in a
diocese is fulfilled. He did not regard the seminary as merely
an institution organized to subject young men destined for the
priesthood to a fixed course of training, moral, intellectual,
and disciplinary, and then send them out upon their mission,
generation after generation, like the output of a factory. Nor
did he consider that the relations between the Seminary and
the priests that were to go forth from its walls should cease
with ordination, or be merely such as exist between an
ordinary college and its alumni. He wished his Seminary to
be a potent moral influence—the very heart and inspiration of
priestly life in his diocese. He wished it to be the *foyer* around
which all his priests, old and young, should gather frequently,
and strengthen among themselves the bonds of zeal, charity,
and fraternal love.

Hence, when after long and patient waiting he felt that the
time had come to build a seminary within the limits of his
own diocese, the plan which he proposed to himself was *not*
to make a vain display of the resources of his diocese; *not* to
eclipse or throw discredit upon other similar institutions already existing in the country; *not* to impose a needless and un-
reasonable burden upon his priests and his people. Not at all!
Nothing could have been further from his mind, or more foreign to his thoughts. But his idea, noble and lofty as it was,

was simply this: To build a seminary that would not only be good enough for the rising generation that were to be educated in it, but that would also *be worthy of the clergy already laboring with him in his diocese*, and from whose example and virtues he had himself derived not only edification, encouragement, and support, but also many of his ideals of true priestly life.

So that in reality it was from *you yourselves*, Rev. Fathers, that he drew his inspiration, and took the measure of the task that he accomplished so perfectly.

In the greatness of his priestly soul he ardently longed to have a fitting place whither you could come and renew your youth at the very fountain of your priestly life.

And God only knows the rapturous joy that inundated his heart and soul when his work was completed and he saw you all assembled in this beautiful chapel for the first time, for your annual Retreat. Surely on that day he felt, in the enjoyment of the first fruits of his great work, that it was well worth all that it had cost of labor, anxiety, and treasure.

And God alone knows the joy that you have felt here, Rev. Fathers, when, kneeling before this beautiful altar, with hearts uplifted and gaze directed toward the Invisible Throne beyond, your eyes have rested upon those blessed words which, on the day of your ordination, were stamped indelibly upon your souls, to remain there forever: Tu es Sacerdos in Æternum! The Seminary was, therefore, according to the noble concept of its founder, to be the welcome rendezvous, the centre of fraternal reunion, for his priests. And it would seem that the Almighty has signified in a striking manner His approval of this part of the great plan, and granted to its pious author the consolation of enjoying some of its fruits. For,

Interior of Chapel of St. Joseph's Seminary
Dunwoodie, N. Y.

while our Archbishop was called to his eternal reward ere the first class that began its full course here reached its completion, he had the happiness of meeting you here many times in the enjoyment of the comforts and blessings which he had striven to procure and prepare for you. May these first fruits continue to be produced in ever-increasing abundance, as a blessing and support to you here on earth, and as an augmentation of his glory and of yours in heaven!

Now, as to the new generations of priests that are to be formed here, I am sure that the desire of his heart was, that they should be *worthy successors of you*, Rev. Fathers, and fitted to deal with whatever new conditions the progress of time, or change of social and intellectual life, may bring about. To the accomplishment of this great end he considered, as I have said, four things absolutely essential: solid piety, thorough discipline, an efficient course of studies, and training in proper ecclesiastical deportment and refinement.

As an inspiration to piety, this chapel, the monument of his personal munificence, stands forth and speaks for itself; while you, Rev. Fathers, from your own experience here within its hallowed precincts, can bear testimony to its efficiency.

As to discipline and intellectual training, no one who knew the Archbishop can hesitate for a moment to believe that his views on this subject were as thorough, far-reaching, and practical as the other portions of his general concept. Of the efficiency with which those views are being actually carried out, I purposely abstain from speaking for obvious reasons. It is for you and others to judge of that by the criterion given us by our Divine Lord Himself, *Ex fructibus cognoscetis*. We cannot ask to be judged by any other; and by it we are willing to stand or to fall.

Finally, as regards training in proper ecclesiastical deportment and the refinement which should make the priest the first of Christian gentlemen, we have in this whole edifice a most excellent object-lesson—which was undoubtedly intended by its founder.

There is, perhaps, no comparison more frequently used by spiritual writers than that of the *material* with the *moral* and *spiritual* edifice. And hence when we examine in detail the various parts of this building, from cellar to garret, the most out-of-the-way nooks and corners, as well as the most prominent halls, reception-rooms, and chapels, and find everywhere the same attention to details, the same care as to materials and workmanship, we see in all this not only a reflection of his own personal character, but also his idea of the care that should be constantly taken, both by those in charge of the Seminary and by the young men themselves, in the building up of *a solid moral edifice—a perfect priestly character.* He wanted no vain, conceited display of learning; still less a vulgar affectation of worldly ways and fashions; nor even solid learning, with gross neglect of social and clerical propriety; nor that erroneous species of selfish piety that excludes zeal, charity, and generosity in the service of God and in the labor for the salvation of souls. Nor did he consider that any amount of learning, culture, exterior decorum, and suavity of manner would make the true priest, so long as serious interior defects were fostered and indulged, or left uncorrected. In a word, he wanted his priests educated here to be at the same time true apostles—men of God—and Christian gentlemen, whose deportment would do honor to their high calling, and make them worthy to enter any door that would be opened to them by the highest or the lowliest in the land, in the spirit of simple faith or out of respect for the *Catholic priesthood.*

This is the great lesson which he wished to have constantly impressed upon those who enter here, even by their material surroundings. And I may say that there are facts upon
record that prove most abundantly that the learning of this
lesson has been seriously insisted upon.

Such then, Rev. Fathers, is, I think, a true though imperfect interpretation of the Archbishop's idea,—grand in its
conception, and admirable in its realization. He has, indeed,
left a noble monument of his love for *the beauty of the house
of God.*

But he has done far more than this.

The world's history is full of instances of men who have
achieved great things for the benefit of mankind, the advancement of learning and of civilization, even of religion, and yet
either their motives or the tenor of their own lives were little
in harmony—often in flagrant contradiction—with the work
which proved so beneficial to others. A Napoleon may enact
wise laws, and prove himself a liberal and enlightened patron
of learning and all the arts of peace, and yet sacrifice the life-
blood and manhood of his nation to a freak of mad, selfish
ambition. A Richelieu may be zealous and efficient in procur-
ing a learned clergy and an able hierarchy, for '' reasons of
state,'' and not be a model ecclesiastic himself. A priest may
build a magnificent church, and acquire a name for business
ability, while allowing his flock to starve for want of spiritual
food, and leaving his debts to be paid by his successor.

Far otherwise was it with the Archbishop. No work did he
ever undertake in the cause of religion that he did not carry
to completion, supporting and fortifying it by the great moral
force of his personal character—his exalted, unfeigned, and
unfailing piety.

We all know that in his private life he lived up to every

principle, practised every virtue, that he professed to stand for in his public works and public utterances. We know his absolute fidelity to all the practices of Catholic piety, from the simple recitation of the Rosary to his daily visit to the Most Blessed Sacrament, and the performance of the most solemn of his episcopal functions. As he lived and moved amongst us he was the personification of the ideal priest. Whether in the midst of his people, or among his seminarians, or surrounded by his clergy, his priestly bearing, which had become a second nature, marked him out as preëminently the *Sacerdos Magnus.*

Who, then, could be more worthy or better fitted to found a seminary? Or who could leave a more precious legacy in the strength of his moral character, and in the edification of his personal, daily life?

Our Archbishop has, therefore, not only planned the Seminary on broad lines, and completed its material construction, but he has *endowed* it with the priceless heritage of his own personality. We may say with all the truth that the figurative expression can convey that his heart is here beneath this altar, and that his spirit abides with us. *Defunctus adhuc loquitur.*

His own work is indeed done; but the seed which he has sown will, with God's blessing, continue to bear fruit so long as his memory is cherished here, his views carried out, and his example imitated.

May you, Rev. Fathers, be spared for many years to reassemble often in this beautiful chapel, to receive new graces and an increase of zeal and love for the "house of God"; and may those who spend here the years of their preparation go forth formed according to the desires and animated with the zeal and devotion of him whose example shall have been constantly before them.

God grant that such may be the case; and if so, how glorious the results to be expected! What a spectacle to contemplate as, in the course of time, you and hundreds of others, aided by the example and emulating the zeal of our founder and patron, having fought the good fight and received your crowns, will stand around the Great Throne, and behold, emblazoned upon his diadem, the plea by which he had won it:

"I have loved, O Lord, the beauty of Thy house, and the place where Thy glory dwelleth."

THE MONTH'S MIND

The Right Reverend Bernard J. McQuaid

Bishop of Rochester

THE MONTH'S MIND

O N Wednesday, the eleventh of June, the Cathedral was again filled with priests and people who came to assist at the Pontifical Mass of Requiem, Month's Mind, for their beloved and regretted Archbishop.

The celebrant of the Mass was the Rt. Rev. Administrator, Monsignor John M. Farley. The Assistant Priest was the Rt. Rev. Mgr. John Edwards. Rev. Charles McCready was the Deacon, and the Very Rev. Albert A. Lings was the Sub-deacon. The Masters of Ceremonies were the Revs. D. J. Curley and J. V. Lewis.

The sermon on the occasion was delivered by the Rt. Rev. Bernard J. McQuaid, Bishop of Rochester, who spoke as follows:

BISHOP McQUAID'S SERMON

BISHOP McQUAID read the following passages from St. Paul to the Thessalonians:

We beseech you, brethren, to know them who labor among you, and are over you in the Lord and admonish you;

That you esteem them more abundantly in charity, for their work's sake. Have peace with them.

And we beseech you, brethren, rebuke the unquiet, comfort the feeble-minded, support the weak, be patient toward all men.

See that none render evil for evil to any man; but ever follow that which is good toward each other, and toward all men.

149

Always rejoice.

Pray without ceasing.

In all things give thanks, for this is the will of God in Christ Jesus concerning you all.

Extinguish not the Spirit.

Despise not prophecies.

But prove all things; hold fast that which is good.

From all appearance of evil refrain yourselves.

And may the God of peace Himself sanctify you in all things; that your whole spirit and soul and body may be preserved blameless in the coming of our Lord Jesus Christ.—First epistle, fifth chapter.

And these verses from the second epistle, third chapter:

And if any man obey not our word by this epistle, note that man, and do not keep company with him, that he may be ashamed.

Yet do not esteem him as an enemy, but admonish him as a brother.

In reading these words of St. Paul, addressed to his disciples, for the most part converts from Judaism and paganism, it struck me that he for whom we pray this day must have permitted those passages of inspired truth to rest in his mind and sink into his heart. The words are addressed to the simple laity, but they are only in another form a repetition of the counsels of the Gospel, or repetitions of the words of Christ Jesus our Lord. We might sum them up in one shorter sentence—"Watch and pray"—watch in labor, in anxiety of soul, but pray, and pray always. In his early childhood he caught the spirit of the Gospel, and in his days of youth imbued soul and mind with eternal truths; and when at length his preparation for the ministry began, they formed a part of his very life and soul. From those earliest days down through his preparation in the school and college and seminary, they guided him in his whole life. In all his work, in all his aspira-

tions, in all his aims, he looked to God, and God's law became
his law; and thus in college and seminary, in the ministry, and
in instructing others and administering the diocese of Newark
in the absence of his Bishop, he was prepared for the administration of this diocese of New York.

New York has had five administrators in its three quarters
of a century of existence. The first was a remarkable man,
though he made no note in the history of the diocese. He was
a man of years when chosen in Rome to come to New York;
he stood high in the ranks of the order of which he was a
member, and was well known to the authorities in Rome and
justly appreciated by them. He came to New York in 1815,
and he found in the State of New York and in the northern
half of New Jersey four priests. By 1822 the number had
grown to eight. Some had their permanent home in the city,
and others were sent out to the most remote parts of the State,
some with knapsacks on their backs, carrying their vestments,
that wherever they found a poor, stray sheep of the fold the
consolations of religion might be brought to such. One was
stationed in Paterson, one in Newark, one at the settlements
along the North River reaching toward Albany, one had his
home in Albany, with what is now the diocese of Albany as
his parish; another was at Utica, and the last was at Rochester.
The Bishop himself, with all his learning and dignified and
princely manners, was a simple parish priest; every work that
falls to the lot of a parish priest fell to him; in a few years,
having brought on his last sickness by attending to the duties
of parochial work, God called him to his rest. But even he, in
those early days when the resources were as nothing and the
people but a handful,—he wrote over to Rome expressing
his regret that it was utterly impossible to establish what his

heart wished to establish—a seminary for the education and training of youth for the priesthood.

He was followed by Bishop Dubois, a man of distinguished parts. He had been obliged to escape from France during the Revolution, and, landing in America at Norfolk, he entered upon the work of the ministry in the diocese of Baltimore. His chief work was the founding of Mount St. Mary's College and Seminary at Emmittsburg. He was a man of eminent learning, of fine accomplishments, and with the zeal of an apostle eating up his soul. As Bishop of New York he found difficulties of many kinds: he was a Frenchman by birth, speaking the English tongue imperfectly; his people, except a few, were not French. Then great contradictions arose before him. In his time, as from the beginning of the Church in the United States, the government of all parishes was in the hands of laymen, who dictated to bishops what should be done. In the archives of the diocese of Rochester we have a letter, addressed by the trustees of the only church then in western New York, a letter characterized by impertinence and insolence and shameful interference with the rights and duties of a bishop. They addressed their Bishop a letter covering four pages, with a species of humility running through it contradicted by their acts. The children of those men would be very sorry to-day to have their fathers' or their grandfathers' letter to their Bishop published. This half-Catholic spirit was the rule in all the dioceses of the United States. John Dubois was a true missionary, a true man of God. His ambition was to establish schools for the young, colleges for the more advanced, and a seminary for priests. He little comprehended the growth of the country; as indeed no one of the five administrators of New York was ever able to foresee its future, and anticipate what was coming. A seminary was built on the Hudson River, on its west bank, at a place called Nyack, difficult of access except by sloop or perhaps steamer. It was burned down in the miserable excitement that then raged over the country during the Maria Monk troubles. Bishop Dubois then chose another place, four hundred miles away, Lafargeville, not far from the St. Lawrence, to be reached from New York, in from eight to ten days, by steamboat, canal-boat, and stage. The climate was inhospitable, the soil poor, and the venture in two years proved a dismal failure.

With the advent of Bishop Hughes as coadjutor to Bishop Dubois, and then administrator, a third administration began.

Administrators are not always rightly judged by their accomplishments; these are often determined by opportunities, demands, and possibilities. The first two administrators have left no monuments behind them but those of zeal, good will, and a true missionary spirit. Circumstances and their surroundings defeated their best endeavors.

When Bishop Hughes came to New York from Philadelphia in 1838, he had already a reputation for ability, manliness of character, great courage and bravery, not disposed to be defiant unnecessarily, but fearing no man when called upon to speak or act.

The Irish immigration was just beginning to surge across the Atlantic, throwing its people in vast numbers upon our shores. A bishop's first duty was to provide priests for these incoming members of his flock, for priests did not come with them, and inducements were not many. Indeed, but a few years before his advent it often happened that parents living in western New York brought their children for baptism to

New York, journeying by stages to Albany and by sloops to New York, a distance of over four hundred miles. A notable instance was that of the late Senator Kernan. The cry in every bishop's ear was, Send us a priest!

One of Bishop Hughes's first acts was to give up Lafargeville and purchase the Rosehill property at Fordham. It was before the extension of the Harlem Railway beyond Harlem. Here, in 1841, he opened a college and seminary under Rev. John McCloskey, afterward Cardinal Archbishop of New York, as its first President. Whatever was left of Lafargeville was brought to Fordham. In 1844 the theological department of Fordham was removed to old St. John's Literary Institute, that then stood where now is the high altar of this Cathedral.

In six months it was brought back to Fordham, and the Lazarists, who had had charge of it, retired from the diocese in 1844. In 1846 the Rosehill property was sold to the Jesuits, with the reservation of the new Seminary building and ten acres of land.

By 1860 Catholics had so increased in number and the demand for priests in proportion that it was determined to establish a seminary for the province of New York, comprising at that time the six New England States, New York and New Jersey. A central point—Troy, New York—was chosen. Large buildings formerly used by the Methodists were bought. Bishop McCloskey of Albany went to Belgium and secured the services of an eminent corps of professors, graduates of Louvain, who, under the presidency of the Very Rev. Dr. Vandenhende, in 1863, opened St. Joseph's Provincial Seminary. Here, for a while, it was thought that a seminary would be founded to answer all the requirements of the growing

Church of Northeast America for many years to come. No one seemed to doubt its permanence and sufficiency for all the wants of the Church. What appeared to be wonderful far-sightedness then was soon seen to be short-sightedness. Yet the Troy Seminary was a blessed boon to the Church, and in its day turned out over seven hundred priests.

By this time it became evident that another problem faced the hierarchy. This was the Christian education of the young of the incoming immigrants. Bishop Dubois and Bishop Hughes, like others at a later date, thought that a compromise with the state might be brought about by which education without positive and distinctive religious instruction might suffice. The price to be paid was the money of the taxpayers. An education without Christ in the school, as attempted in the old Cathedral School, proved a lamentable failure, but a service-able lesson. It was then that Bishop Hughes was led to declare publicly that the day had come for the Catholic school to pre-cede the Church. With this thought in mind, he turned all his energies toward making the Catholic school possible every-where. Brothers and sisters of various communities were in-vited to the diocese, and encouragement was freely lent for growth and successful work. There is a change to-day from that first colony of religious, children of Mother Seton, herself a convert and child of the diocese, baptized in old St. Peter's Church on Barclay Street, and the multitudes engaged in Catholic schools before Bishop Hughes's death in 1864.

Times had been stormy under John Hughes. Why not? The Maria Monk troubles had disgraced the country and cut to the heart the timid Catholics of America. This outbreak was followed by the Native American disturbances and riots; four or five mobs at different times had gathered to destroy the old Cathedral on Mott Street. The last time I witnessed an assault upon it the Mayor was there, and artillery, cavalry, and regiments of infantry, to protect the Church in New York city. They were, I say, troublous times when John Hughes reigned, who found it more difficult to defend the Church's rights because of the timidity of his own people. The Catholics of New York were afraid to hold up their heads. They were few in number, but sufficiently numerous to make themselves felt had they had the courage of men. But Bishop Hughes defied all those enemies; he defied the press, that without exception was bitter against him, that reviled him day by day, that misrepresented his actions, that excited the lowest bigots of the country to rise up against the Catholic Church. His heart never failed, his courage never gave way, not even when struck in the back by his own people; not even when a trusted member of his flock took sides against him privately, and caused the politicians at Albany to withdraw from their intention to render just rights to the Catholics of the country. Often had I occasion to listen to Catholics out in rural districts, who, having read the New York papers—chiefly the New York "Herald"—had their minds poisoned by those attacks, who had grown ashamed of him who of all men that had ever lived in the country was best able from his bravery of soul to lead us. His own friends, I say, stabbed him in the back, and he went to his grave not knowing the names of the traitors. But when the storm was passing away and the merits of the man were about to be thoroughly appreciated, when he was called upon by the government of the country to assist them in securing peace in Mexico, and later on to hold back the interference of European powers during our desperate Civil War, his merits were better understood.

Then came the gentle reign of Cardinal McCloskey, a prince among princes, a man of learning and fine parts, devoted to his church work, but well adapted to smooth over the asperities of the past and quell opposition by the meekness and gentleness of his manner. He took up the work at the very beginning of his administration which John Hughes had initiated. Bishop Hughes showed more foresight than any one that has ever had the care of this diocese. Some of you may remember that Sunday afternoon when we met here for the placing of the corner-stone of this church. The location was far out in the fields, one might say; they were only beginning to open other streets than Third Avenue and the Bloomingdale Road in the upper part of the city. It was a warm afternoon, very dusty, and every one thought that John Hughes was visionary. The idea of placing a cathedral here! They criticized him, and they found fault; and when at last he succeeded in raising $70,000 of the $100,000 which he proposed to raise we were all filled with amazement that so much money could be found among our Catholic people. He then wisely left the foundation walls covered up. When Bishop McCloskey came our people had increased largely in number, churches were spread over the island, the financial resources of our people had also grown, and he was able to go on and complete this Cathedral.

The first four bishops were eminent, distinguished men; yet how little they accomplished in the beginning! John Connolly, first Bishop, next to nothing, except the one good work of carefully looking after all the members of the flock that were here under his jurisdiction. John Dubois did more, for population and resources had grown. They made efforts to establish ecclesiastical undertakings upon a right basis, but their accomplishments were not many. John Connolly brought the first Sisters of Charity to this island. They were the children of Mother Seton. She had, just a few years before, formed a colony of pious women for work among the poor, and especially in the schools. Bishop Dubois increased the number of those that were thus to work, and by the time Bishop Hughes came into action it was necessary to widen the boundaries and bring in more help of men and of women; and so religious communities were multiplied. But not one of them had any conception of the future of this Church of New York.

So I say to-day, in view of the past, there is no one living that would presume to speak of the future of this diocese in the course of the next fifty years. Where is it to end? What is to be the outcome of its possibilities in the next fifty years, if the past fifty years, under adverse circumstances, have brought forth so much?

At the end of the fourth administration the fifth ruling power came into play. This was the illustrious dead, whose memory we honor this day, Archbishop Corrigan. His preparation was a most excellent one: from his childhood a young saint, in college a bright and successful student, in the American College at Rome, where his theological course was completed, crowned at its close with the doctorate; then for four years after his return to America at Seton Hall College, Professor of Dogmatic Theology and of Sacred Scripture. I speak of what I know well. No young student in that Seminary was more observant of rule than its director; no one there kept more faithfully the hours of study and of rest than Dr. Corrigan. In those four years his life was beautiful, simple, truly pious, devoted to his work and to God; no evidence was there of any desire ever to distinguish himself or to rise above others, warranted by his superior ability; no evidence in those four

years other than that he meant to be professor, there to live
and there to die. When at length, in the providence of God,
he was called to take charge of the College and Seminary, in
succession to the former President, his Bishop, when spoken
to, said: "I cannot place him there; he is only a girl." One
who knew him well answered: "He may be a girl in appearance, but he is a man of God in his soul and as firm as a rock."
And so he was almost forced into office as President of the College and Seminary and Vicar-General of the diocese.

In three or four years Bishop Bayley of Newark was removed to Baltimore, and a successor had to be found. When
the name of Dr. Corrigan was mentioned there was a smile on
every one's face. "How can we think of making him a
bishop?" His own Bishop did not desire him for his successor; quite the contrary; he had another choice. But when the
matter came before the Board of Bishops I spoke from my certain knowledge and assured the bishops that they had little
comprehension of the capacity and the learning and the
strength of will power of that mere boy, as they regarded him;
and upon the pledge of my word in ten minutes he was placed
first on the list. He then spent four years to prepare himself
in New Jersey for coming to New York. They were four years
of most excellent discipline. He learned to do everything except to construct a building. That he never learned. He
learned how to organize men, to use them to do his work, systematically, orderly, according to rule, seeking to throw upon
them the responsibility of work for which they were well
adapted and he was not adapted at all. In New Jersey, during
his years there, you might call him almost a missionary bishop,
going from place to place with the same sweet simplicity of
manner. When at last he was chosen for New York by the

Archbishop—Cardinal Archbishop McCloskey—though still very young-looking in appearance and very young in years, too, he came here not unprepared, but he came here to find difficulties that he never dreamed of, that did not show themselves in the lifetime of Cardinal McCloskey, whose princely dignity and past record in Albany and New York had held in check slumbering disappointments.

There never was a man holding the office of Bishop against whom such opposition should have arisen. He had his duty to do and he did it. In the doing of it if troubles broke out there was never a moment's anger in his soul, and I know of what I am speaking. There was grief that the humble laity might be scandalized and some might break away from the fold. But his duty was clear; he had one great advantage— he knew his theology; he knew not only his catechism, which the humblest member of the flock may know, but he knew profound, scholastic theology; he knew it in all its application to changes of times and circumstances; he had learned it in the source, I might say, of Catholic truth and teaching—in Rome itself. In his mind he thought as God's Church thought, and in his soul he felt as the apostles of old felt, or as those great bishops of the Eastern and the Western Churches in their days of trial and persecution and martyrdom felt. They grieved that God should be offended by the unguided and disorderly; but they held to God's truth, as their conscience obliged them to hold steadfast to their faith. In those days your Archbishop had one friend, one upon whom he relied, one before whom he went at every moment, one to whom he could open his heart, and that friend was Jesus Christ in the tabernacle. Day and night he gave way to prayer, and no angry look ever came from his countenance. He felt for others; he had no enemies except the devil and his works; no man could be his enemy except in upholding the cause of wrong or of doctrine untrue to the Gospel of Christ and of Christ's own Church.

He is dead now—cut off in the prime of his life, just when the world's crown of glory was being woven for his head. His life as administrator of New York was one of toil and labor. With the authority of a father speaking to his child, how often I almost lost patience with him when I saw that his mode of life was breaking him down and would prematurely end his days unless he paid some regard to the laws of nature. A man must relax at times, for no man can stand the strain of early days, when fifty and fifty-five years have passed, without taking occasional rest. There was no rest for him; he would try to combine the work of his duty with rest. That was never rest. When he left the city for a short vacation his business followed him wherever he went. The last time he came to Rochester I told him before coming that unless he could leave his business behind him it was no use to come to my beautiful and quiet summer resort. "Why not," I said, "take example from the venerable Archbishop of Boston? He leaves letters and telegrams and everything behind him, and gives his mind a few weeks of absolute rest." I was blunt enough to say: "Indeed, if you cannot do this you had better not come at all." He came, and for once left that mill of toil behind him. I only know of two or three letters that came to him, and they were written by some pious nuns who ought to have prayed for him and kept their little troubles to themselves.

I have trespassed upon your time, but there are two or three things I would like to refer to, two or three striking and notable events of his life. I do not speak about the wonderful works he has accomplished here in the city and all through the diocese. You know all these things; you know how he bravely dared to plan and carry out that noble Seminary at Dunwoodie; you know how anxious he was that your children should all be gathered into Catholic schools; and you of the clergy who last met with him know that he announced his will with regard to building school-houses, when he declared that every one who within two years had not established his Catholic school should give him in writing the reasons therefor. With him it was a matter of conscience. He understood that no bishop can be negligent in his duties of caring for the young without sinning before God; and with no thought of death in the near future he wanted not to have his soul burdened with the crime of depriving the young through any neglect on his part or on the part of his priests, of that Christian education to which they were entitled by the laws of God Himself. When first I heard of his death, or of his approaching death, the thought came to my mind: How good God was to him, that although all through his administration he had sought to provide for the young of the flock, yet among his last acts was his admirable promulgation to his clergy, "We must have schools for our children." He knew the past of this diocese, how Bishop Dubois and then Bishop Hughes sought a combination with the city—a combination, an arrangement, a compromise with an unbelieving state—that the city officials would pay their money if we would put Christ and the crucifix and the Blessed Mary and all the saints and God out of our school-houses, and permit no mention of God or Christ. I felt that at last, before he died, he did a noble act that covered over everything, if ever there was a weakness in the man's life or character, by this noble pronouncement in behalf of Christian education.

There are two little incidents to which I shall refer, as they illustrate his character so beautifully. I sat near him on that memorable evening when his silver jubilee as Bishop was celebrated in the largest hall of your city, and I listened to men of eminent ability, clerics and laymen, Catholic and Protestant, pouring out testimony and tributes of excellence, of worth and of virtue, upon the head of that humble little man. I tried to read his countenance. I wondered how he could listen to it; no proud man could. He listened to it all absolutely unmoved, just as a saint might listen to such praise of another. As I scanned his countenance I could see no exultation of heart, no joy of spirit; he was simply passive. When he rose to speak he gave due thanks to all who had been so kind to him; he thanked them for that noble gift of $250,000 coming from his priests and his people; he thanked them for all that they had done. The next evening we met in this church; and here were 5000 children, the pick and representatives of 40,000 Catholic children in the Catholic parochial schools of this city. He ascended this pulpit and addressed those children. There was joy of soul; then he was uplifted; then beautiful passages from the Scriptures and the Fathers came to his mind; they were his children. The sweet, innocent ones were his children; they told of his success, of the labors of his priests and his people. He was a happy man that evening. I will not say he was never so happy before; but he was grateful and glad, and that outbursting of the soul overflowing with joy because of what was being done for the little ones of his flock, shone upon his countenance and lighted it up.

The second incident is this: Some years ago your Archbishop's loyalty to the Holy See was called in question. We

who were behind the scenes knew what was passing and under
stood well how it came to pass. We had read the newspapers—
some Catholic ones were the worst. Through covert insinua-
tions that were believed in many places your Archbishop was
charged with lack of loyalty to Rome, and he was called on to
make public profession of his faith and loyalty. Of all the
bishops that these United States had ever known he was the
last to be put to such a test; he was the last to have his faith
and loyalty called in question. I never could have gone
through what he so gently and so sweetly did in his simple way.
He came into this pulpit, like the saint that he was: he had
little, if I remember rightly, to say about himself; he did not
seem concerned even that he should be assailed; but that which
troubled him was that this diocese of New York should ever
have its loyalty to the Holy See called in question. So he
recounted the acts of the past, how this bishop and the other
had stood; it was not to defend himself, but the clergy and the
people of this diocese, that he spoke those beautiful words, worthy of any confessor of the faith in all time to come. He knew
his religion; he knew the authority of the Church of Rome;
no doubt ever crossed his mind; he was not afraid to announce
its teachings whenever occasion offered; he feared not the
world. He never would yield one iota to win the applause of
a non-Catholic community; he won it, but he won it by the nobility of his character, his honorable upholding of what was
right and true; he won it as a man might win it and not have
to bow his head through shame.

His administration has come to a close. But what will be
the administration of the next fifty years? From the four
priests and a bishop in 1815 to the two bishops and seven
hundred and more priests in 1902! Europe stands amazed at

America. Especially do those countries stand amazed at the growth of the city of New York, destined soon to be the money centre of the world, the commercial centre of America, and its industrial centre at the same time in material concerns. The world is forging ahead rapidly; all the traditions of the past are thrown to one side. The empires of Europe are startled by what they behold; and when men take the trouble to come here and patiently study the workings of the Catholic Church in this city and in this diocese, they too are startled. We are not so hampered by tradition and the circumstances of other countries; we are freer; we are a braver people; our religion lies down deep in the heart; no longer are we ashamed of it; to-day every means is used to push that religion forward, that the whole world may know what is this religion of Christ. What is to be the future of this diocese and this province of New York? Little did Bishop Connolly do in his day; he had no opportunity. Little did Dubois do; he had no opportunity. But the opportunities and possibilities are before you; before you the priests and laymen of the most important diocese in America, if not in Christendom. Yours are the opportunities and possibilities of the future. You will be judged by what you shall have accomplished, and by what you shall have left undone.

Now I sum up all in what, I think, is the most pleasant feature in the life and the work of our good Archbishop Corrigan. He was here busy about all the temporal affairs of the diocese, holding meetings, transacting business, approving of this and correcting that. There are other men in this city who are busy the same way, but that work in which he was most of all engaged, that which chiefly enlisted his soul, that which in his mind was paramount in the building up of the Church in this diocese, was the education of his priests, so that not only should their minds be filled with all ecclesiastical learning, but that every one of them should be endowed with a spiritual character and lead a spiritual life. It is noble to inform the mind and fill the soul with courage; it is noble to preach and work for the people, to build up the Church; but what Archbishop Corrigan wanted, above all, was to make his priests superior men, priestly priests, who would think and talk and act like priests everywhere, so that when out among the people every one would know that they were priests, priests of the great diocese of New York, with nothing boyish or careless about them, always dignified and self-respecting. Above all things, he desired them to be men of prayer—men devoted to their work.

The ambition of your late Archbishop was most praiseworthy. Why God did not permit him to live longer and carry out his grand ideas, God only knows. Perhaps he can do more for you in heaven than here on earth; perhaps his powerful intercession before the throne of Eternal Mercy will benefit priests and people more effectually than his presence among you, and enable his successor to take up his unfinished work and carry it forward to completion. He was planning a preparatory seminary that would gather within its class-rooms the pick of the diocese—the chosen ones—the very ones on whom the hand of God seemed to rest—and by special care and training prepare them from their young days for entrance into the Seminary at Dunwoodie; thus guaranteeing a priesthood for New York unsurpassed in the world—a priesthood that would make its influence for good felt the whole United States over.

Pray pardon the coldness of my language, for I have not

dared let my heart speak. To no one has the death of the Archbishop brought more sorrow than to me. He was to me and to all his suffragans a most brotherly prelate, always patient and helpful. To me in particular, who watched his career from his boyhood to the closing of his life, he lived the life of a saint, and died the death of a saint.

RESOLUTIONS

Specimen of the Illuminated Resolutions of the Board of Aldermen of the City of New York

RESOLUTIONS

CITY OF NEW YORK,
OFFICE OF MAYOR,
July 8, 1902.

Right Reverend and Dear Sir:

In handing you the engrossed copy of the resolutions adopted by the Board of Aldermen of the City of New York in memory of the late Archbishop Corrigan, I take the opportunity to express anew my own sense of loss in the death of the late Archbishop, and to assure you of the high appreciation in which he was held by men of every creed for his unassuming and useful life. The members of his own Church, in their own peculiar loss, have had, I am sure, the sympathy of all the people.   Yours very truly,

SETH LOW,
Mayor.

To
Right Rev. JOHN M. FARLEY, D.D.,
Administrator.

BOARD OF ALDERMEN OF THE CITY OF NEW YORK

Whereas, God in His omnipotent wisdom has called to Himself MICHAEL AUGUSTINE CORRIGAN, Archbishop of New York, distinguished prelate, incorruptible patriot, and tender shepherd to a flock numbering a million of people; and,

171

Whereas, Archbishop Corrigan, no common type of man, by his wise direction, his thorough scholarship, his saintly life, and his sterling attributes commanded the reverence, affection, respect, and love, not only of his own co-religionists, but of all classes of citizens and residents of this country, irrespective of religious ties; and,

Whereas, His conservative and enlightened influence was always strenuously exerted for good in behalf of his native country and of the City of New York, which he loved so well; the high status enjoyed by him in the Church of which he was so noble an exemplar, his abstemious, frugal life, and his wide and universal charity to all, made him, if not the most conspicuous, at least one of the greatest characters in this metropolis of the Western Hemisphere; therefore, be it

Resolved, That we, the members of the Board of Aldermen of the City of New York, mindful of the courageous, heroic, and patriotic sacrifices of the Most Rev. Michael Augustine Corrigan of the diocese of New York, hereby express our admiration and appreciation of his unsullied life, his ever outstretched hand to charity, and his patient bearing with the long-suffering and afflicted; and deem him a meet and worthy successor of the militant and noble John Hughes, first Archbishop of New York, and his gracious Eminence the late Cardinal John McCloskey, and hereby give utterance to our sincere sorrow at his early death; and, be it further

Resolved, That a special Committee of seven members be appointed by the President of this Board to make arrangements for suitable participation in the obsequies; that his

Honor the Mayor be and he is requested to display the flags at half-mast on the City Hall from now until the day of the funeral, and that this Board attend the ceremonies in a body; that the City Clerk be and he is hereby authorized and directed to cause a copy of this preamble and resolutions to be suitably engrossed and duly authenticated, and transmit a copy of the same to the authorities of the Roman Catholic Church in this city.

In Board of Aldermen, May 6, 1902, unanimously adopted by a rising vote, all the members elected voting in favor thereof.

TRUSTEES OF ST. PATRICK'S CATHEDRAL, NEW YORK

The Board of Trustees of St. Patrick's Cathedral, at a special meeting called on May 6, 1902, at its offices, in the City of New York, ordered the following minute of its proceedings to be published in the newspapers of the city on the day of the funeral of the late Archbishop of New York:

The Most Rev. Michael Augustine Corrigan was, by virtue of his office, president of this Board, which has charge of the temporalities of the Cathedral, and the members, in the discharge of their duties having been in frequent and close intercourse with him during his life, make this reverent and affectionate offering to his memory.

He was a Christian gentleman, possessed of great intellectual abilities, great learning, and great power of will, and would have shone highly in any walk of life which he might have chosen. But these characteristics were the lesser part of his nature, and his message to the world would have been un-delivered if his spiritual energy had not an opportunity to dis-play itself in its deep and varied magnificence.

Coming into office at a time when our civilization was appar-ently triumphing through its material energies alone, he exer-cised his influence over the forces within his jurisdiction, mainly through a gentle and meek spiritual power, strong in its faith, ardent in its hope, and self-forgetting in its charity.

And it came to pass that during his life as archbishop the period of great material development and influence in the arch-diocese was coincident with and caused by a period of greater spiritual devotion on the part of its head.

By his accomplishments he emphasized the truth that the Church progresses in the world not through material aggran-dizement, but by its equal care for all of its children, and that the greatest force in life, whether religious, civil, or political, is love—love of God, love of country, and love of our fellow-man.

THE ROMAN CATHOLIC ORPHAN ASYLUM

The Board of Managers of the Roman Catholic Orphan Asylum in the City of New York inscribes this minute in the proceed-ings of a special meeting held for that purpose on May 6, 1902:

The death of our beloved Archbishop, though a great per-sonal bereavement to each member of this Board, has a wider significance, as it causes an irreparable loss not alone to charity, religion, and the state, but to Christianity itself. His efforts were directed not only to the amelioration of the condition of

The Roman Catholic Orphan Asylum of New York. The New Building (Boys' Department)

Kingsbridge, N. Y., 1901

the downtrodden and the poor, but to the maintenance of the highest ideals of religion, exerting by them an extended influence on good government and the perpetuation of the institutions of our country. Though his heart and sympathy went out to the poor and the unfortunate, his sense of right and justice made him an inflexible conservator of vested interests and the rights of property. He was strongly imbued with the sentiment of patriotism, which it was his constant effort to have inculcated in all the schools under his jurisdiction.

We recognize in him not only a great prelate, but a great man, who may well be described as a model of every virtue which adorns a priest and a citizen. Conspicuous for his firmness, courage, and justice, he was no less noted for gentleness, meekness, and mercy. On the occasion of his silver jubilee the public expression of affection he received from the entire community, irrespective of creed, evidenced the high place he had attained in the esteem of men, and those who knew his self-sacrifice, devotion to duty, and priestly life may confidently believe that he merited an eternal crown.

We who have been intimately associated in one of the many charities dear to his heart—the care of orphan children—feel most deeply the loss of his wise counsel and guidance, and sympathize with the orphans who are deprived of his fatherly care. As president of this Board for more than twenty years, he assiduously labored for the comfort and happiness of those committed to its care, and one of the crowning acts of his life, which in a special manner emphasized his loving solicitude in their behalf, came at the very end in the erection and completion of a permanent home for them, which will long remain as a splendid monument built by him to religion and charity.

Mindful as we are of his great and important work for the

community in which he lived and the Christian religion, we deem it especially appropriate that there should be entered upon our records a minute expressive of his invaluable services to the homeless orphans, and of their and our sentiments of esteem and affection, and of our sense of the irreparable loss sustained by his untimely death; and as a testimonial of our loving respect it is ordered that this minute be spread upon our records, that our asylum be draped in mourning for the space of thirty days, and that the members of this Board attend his funeral in a body.

THE PARTICULAR COUNCIL
SOCIETY OF ST. VINCENT DE PAUL
IN THE CITY OF NEW YORK

Whereas, It has pleased Almighty God in His infinite wisdom to call unto Himself our revered and beloved Archbishop, whose whole life was a living example of the virtues of humility, patience, and charity; whose first thought was the love and glory of God, and next to it his love for and interest in the poor, in whom he always saw Christ his Master; whose hand and heart were ever ready to aid struggling youth as well as to provide homes for the orphan, the aged and infirm; whose life work is a monument which will perpetuate his name to posterity; and,

Whereas, Our society has lost a warm friend and a wise counsellor, whose interest in all of its various works was well known to all our members, who strongly indorsed and actively supported all our special works; and,

Whereas, Through his cordial coöperation our society has become larger and a very prominent factor in the field of charity; and

Whereas, By his regular attendance at our meetings and his many words of kindly advice, he encouraged the many conferences in the observance of our rules, and pointed out to us the proper spirit in which we should conduct our most important work, the visitation and relief of the poor in their homes; and,

Whereas, In his death the Church and the faithful within this archdiocese, as well as in the country at large, have suffered a severe loss;

Resolved, That the prayers of our society be offered for his eternal rest and be continued at our regular meetings for a period of thirty days.

THE SUPERIOR COUNCIL,
SOCIETY OF ST. VINCENT DE PAUL

Whereas, Almighty God, in His Divine Providence, has called away our beloved Archbishop, who for so many years bore the cares and shaped the destinies of this archdiocese, during which period, in every act of his busy life as priest of God and archbishop, he set an example of simple faith, noble self-sacrifice, infinite patience, and devotion to duty that compelled the unstinted admiration and love of all who knew him; and

Whereas, No work of charity within his vast archdiocese ever failed of his encouragement and support, always finding him ready with cheering word and helping hand; and

Whereas, In the death of our beloved Archbishop the Superior Council of the Society of St. Vincent de Paul in New York has sustained a heavy loss, in that he was at all times active in furthering by word and deed the work of the society, lending the aid of his influence over the entire circumscription; therefore, be it

Resolved, That the members of the council attend his funeral in a body; and be it further

Resolved, That a circular letter be addressed to each conference of the circumscription, asking the prayers of the members for the repose of the soul of one of the most devoted friends and advocates the society ever had.

BOARD OF MANAGERS OF THE NEW YORK CATHOLIC PROTECTORY

At a special meeting of the Board of Managers of the New York Catholic Protectory, the following resolutions were adopted:

Grieved in heart and with heads bowed in resignation to the will of the Eternal Father, the Board of Managers of the New York Catholic Protectory unite in the general sorrow and deeply mourn the loss of the Most Reverend Archbishop, Michael Augustine Corrigan, beloved for his personal virtues, reverenced for his charity, revered and respected, admired and appreciated for his piety, courage, and learning; great as a prelate, great as a citizen, and, withal, an exemplar of modesty and humility.

The suavity of his manners and the forcefulness of his dignity have brought forth abundant and fruitful results in the administration of the diocese, and the New York Catholic Protectory, upon which he bestowed a solicitous care, has received its full share of those many blessings resulting from his unsparing devotion to his flock; therefore, be it

Resolved, That we, the members of the Board of Managers of the New York Catholic Protectory, mindful of the benefits received through the Most Reverend Archbishop, by reason of the wisdom of his guidance, the gentleness of his supervision, and the mildness of his authority in the affairs of the Protectory, do solemnly express on this sad occasion our great appreciation of the pious and paternal power by him exercised over us.

While offering to the Almighty our most fervent prayers for the repose of the soul of our deceased pastor, may we hope that our management of the Protectory, so benignly influenced by his example in life, will still remain so influenced by his memory in death; further

Resolved, That the members of the Board of Managers attend the funeral in a body.

MISSION OF THE IMMACULATE VIRGIN

At a special meeting of the Board of Trustees of the Mission of the Immaculate Virgin, held at No. 2 Lafayette Place on May 7, 1902, the following resolutions were adopted:

Whereas, In His infinite wisdom our Almighty Father has taken from us our most beloved president, the Most Rev. Michael A. Corrigan.

Whereas, He had always been identified most particularly with the work of the Mission, by his constant presence at the meetings of this Board, by his gentle and kindly advice at the same, and by the keen interest which he ever manifested in all matters pertaining to the advantage of poor children and the success of the Mission.

Resolved, As true Catholics we bow in humble submission to the will of God.

Resolved, That the Board of Trustees attend the Pontifical Mass of Requiem.

Resolved, That the Mission of the Immaculate Virgin be draped in mourning for thirty days.

Resolved, That on Monday, the eleventh of May, Masses of Requiem be offered up in each of the chapels of the Mission of the Immaculate Virgin.

XAVIER ALUMNI SODALITY

The council of the Xavier Alumni Sodality, at a special meeting held on May 8, 1902, to take action on the death of the Most Rev. Michael Augustine Corrigan, D.D., Archbishop of New York, adopted the following resolution:

Resolved, That the members of the Xavier Alumni Sodality join in the universal grief at the death of our revered Archbishop, but are consoled by the memory of his life, overflowing with deeds of charity, love, and devotion to his people. While at all times wisely maintaining and fostering the Church

in his care, and aiding and advancing every cause for the good
of society, he has left the example of a life of a great prelate,
a devoted priest, and a noble citizen.

THE CATHOLIC CLUB

It is our sad duty to announce the death of our beloved
Archbishop and benefactor, the Most Rev. Michael Augustine
Corrigan, D.D., Archbishop of New York. We can only add
our voice in the universal chorus of praise and love going up
from the community for the character and work of our late
departed friend.

The Catholic Club was especially honored by the confidence
and coöperation of our dear Archbishop. He manifested on
every occasion his personal and official interest in the work of
our organization. In many instances he introduced numbers
into the club and whenever possible appeared in person at our
club events.

He was the highest type of a Christian gentleman; the model
priest and bishop.

May perpetual light shine upon him.

---

*At a special meeting of the Board of Management of the Catho-
lic Club of the City of New York, held May 6, 1902, the following resolutions were unanimously adopted:*

Whereas, Realizing the loss which is ours, and appreciating
the gain which is his, we mourn the death while we glory in the
triumph of our revered and beloved Archbishop, Most Rev.

Michael Augustine Corrigan, D.D., whose faithful soul, on the night of the fifth of May, answered the call from the throne of God;

Whereas, In his death a chieftain of the Church has fallen in the vanguard of service to God and country, where, with Christian humility, but steadfast as the Rock, he stood for the faith of Him Who taught, " To Cæsar the things that are Cæsar's, and to God the things that are God's"; and

Whereas, During his apostolic career he maintained the standard of Catholicism in the high place where his illustrious predecessor had set it, and fostering every influence that made for the advancement of religion and society, he aided and honored the Catholic Club of New York with his counsel and friendship.

Therefore, Be it resolved, That we, the members of the Catholic Club, bowing with resignation to the mandate which takes from his children in the faith a father, desire to give expression to sentiments of profound reverence and sorrow for our departed prelate.

Resolved, That the most fitting tribute which we, as Catholic laymen, can pay to his memory is devotion to the Christian patriotism which he professed and fidelity to the truths of religion planted by him in the field where he fell, surrounded by harvests which he had reaped for Christianity.

Resolved, That the club house of the Catholic Club be appropriately draped in mourning during a period of thirty days from the fifth inst.; that all social functions at the club be cancelled during said period; that these resolutions be spread upon the club's records, and that a copy be transmitted to the administrator of the archdiocese of New York.

CATHOLIC HOME BUREAU

The following resolutions were adopted at a meeting of the Board of Directors of the Catholic Home Bureau, held Tuesday, May 6, 1902:

Whereas, The dawn of this day has brought us the news that Almighty God has called unto Himself our beloved Archbishop, wherefore our affliction is heavy and our grief profound; let it be

Resolved, That we give expression in the minutes of this meeting to the sentiments of love and filial affection which we cherished for him, of admiration for his saintly life, of satisfaction over the successful results of his wise archiepiscopal administration for nearly a score of years, and above all to the sentiments of gratitude which we must ever feel for his noble attitude of encouragement in the foundation of the form of charity to which we are more particularly devoted, and for the public recognition and strong support which his enlightened mind and noble heart prompted him to give it; and let it be

Resolved, Also, that in entering upon our minutes this tribute to our beloved Hierarch, we mean it to be an incentive now to the prayers of ourselves and our wards for the repose of his soul, and ever after a memorial in our archives to the great and good founder, Michael Augustine Corrigan.

HOLY NAME SOCIETY

Whereas, It has pleased Almighty God in His wisdom to take from us our beloved Archbishop, Michael Augustine Corrigan, thus bringing to an earthly end the life of a great bishop of the Church, a learned theologian and scholar, a gentle, holy man; and,

Whereas, Our late Archbishop had endeared himself to all the members of his flock by the kindliness of his manner, earnestness in his discourses, the sincerity and sweetness of his character, and the Christian piety and humility of his life; had won the admiration and respect of the entire community, of every shade of religious belief, by the dignity with which he maintained his position, as well as the intensity of his patriotism and the strong love of country he manifested at all times; had earned the thanks of the faithful by his untiring efforts in the cause of religion and Holy Mother Church, so that his charge expanded to enormous proportions and became the home of every active religious movement,—his whole life and character, aims and achievements, redounding to the greater honor and glory of God and the lasting credit of our American institutions; therefore, be it

Resolved, By the Archdiocesan Union of the Holy Name Society, composed of seventy branches, representing sixteen thousand Catholics of the archdiocese of New York, that we hereby express the deep sympathy we feel with the grief of the archdiocese in being deprived of a noble pastor and a loving father; of the city and nation in the loss of an exemplary man and citizen, an American by birth, training, and sentiment;

and of the Church militant at the loss of a great commander in the battle against the forces of error and evil; and,

Resolved, That we hereby express our own most deep and heartfelt feelings in the death of our Archbishop, our sorrow and grief, the keen sense of personal loss, the aching void left in our hearts, the shadow of anguish and mourning cast over our lives; and,

Resolved, That as he was a faithful disciple of the Master, and strove zealously for the salvation of souls, the prayers of our members be offered to God for the repose of his own soul and the reaping of the heavenly reward he so richly earned; and,

Resolved, That, as a slight tribute to his memory, these resolutions be entered on the minutes this sixteenth day of June, 1902.

NEW YORK STATE COUNCIL, CATHOLIC BENEVOLENT LEGION

Whereas, It has pleased Almighty God in His infinite wisdom to take unto Himself, from the scene of his labor and activity, the Most Rev. Michael Augustine Corrigan, D.D., Archbishop of New York; and,

Whereas, In the death of Archbishop Corrigan the Church in America has lost one of its brightest ornaments, the nation one of its most loyal and patriotic citizens, the Catholic Benevolent Legion one of its staunchest friends and patrons; therefore, be it

Resolved, That the New York State Council of the Catholic Benevolent Legion, in its twentieth annual convention assembled, with our co-religionists throughout the country and the world, deplore the death of this respected prelate, and testify to the deep and earnest interest he had in the Catholic Benevolent Legion and all kindred organizations; we testify to the earnestness, piety, learning, and zeal which characterized his life and the administration of the high and exalted duties he was called upon to administer.

Resolved, That a copy of these resolutions be forwarded to the administrator of the diocese and spread upon the minutes of this convention.

THE ALUMNI OF THE AMERICAN COLLEGE

Resolutions adopted at the alumni meeting of the American College of the Roman Catholic Church of the United States, Rome, Italy, held at the New Willard Hotel, Washington, D. C., Wednesday, May 14, 1902:

Whereas, Almighty God has taken to Himself our beloved and most distinguished alumnus, the Most Rev. Michael Augustine Corrigan, Archbishop of New York; and

Whereas, He was from the beginning a staunch and devoted friend and zealous supporter of the College, and of this association; and,

Whereas, We deeply feel and mourn his loss as peculiarly personal to ourselves; therefore, be it

Resolved, first, That the alumni of the American College at Rome express their sincere sorrow at his death, and offer their heartfelt sympathy to his clergy, who have lost their saintly, learned, and loving pastor and father.

Resolved, second, That we extend to his relatives our profound condolence.

Resolved, third, That a copy of these resolutions, suitably engraved, be forwarded to the American College in Rome, and to the archiepiscopal curia of New York City.

THE UNITED STATES
CATHOLIC HISTORICAL SOCIETY

At a meeting of the Executive Council of the United States Catholic Historical Society, held June 18, 1902, the following preamble and resolutions were adopted:

Whereas, In His divine wisdom and providence, Almighty God has called to Himself the Most Rev. Michael A. Corrigan, Archbishop of New York; and

Whereas, The late Archbishop was for many years the Honorary President of the United States Catholic Historical Society; therefore, be it

Resolved, That we record our sense of the great loss we have suffered by the death of one who, by word and deed, again and again proved the esteem in which he held the purposes and objects of our society.

By his influence and by his example he aided us in the important work of preserving and recording the history of the Catholic Church in our country.

His presence at our public meetings was a continued evidence of the interest he took in our proceedings. His kindly and wise advice, especially at times when our society was contending with vital difficulties, gave most inspiring encouragement to our efforts.

To every number of our "Historical Studies and Records" Archbishop Corrigan contributed valuable papers, which often rescued from oblivion facts and incidents of the greatest interest and importance in the history of the American Church.

Resolved, That we share the sentiments of regret, of respect, and of veneration which the death of the great Archbishop has elicited, not only in his own archdiocese, but in the whole of the United States, and, indeed, in the whole world.

Resolved, That these resolutions be entered in the minutes of our society proceedings, as a perpetual memorial of a most distinguished member, and that a copy thereof be duly prepared and attested and sent to the archives of the Archdiocese of New York, and that a copy be likewise sent to the mourning relatives, in whose grief we deeply sympathize.

THE CATHOLIC KNIGHTS OF AMERICA

The supreme officers of the Catholic Knights of America desire to place on the records of our order an expression of deepest sorrow at the death of our distinguished brother, the eminent Archbishop of the City of New York, Most Rev. M. A. Corrigan.

For four years he was the supreme spiritual director of our

order, and always manifested an interest in our affairs, enhanced by the fact that the Catholic Knights of America was the only Catholic fraternal organization of which he was an active member.

For twelve years his name occupied the first place on the roll of Branch 258. He cheerfully accepted the place of honor assigned to him by our New York brothers on the night of their silver jubilee celebration, the thirtieth of April; but the fatal illness had come upon him, and he was unable to attend. His vacant chair was covered with roses expressive of the warmth of the love of the Knights for the absent one.

His stupendous labors as the head of the greatest archdiocese of America are plainly evident in the many monuments erected in the cause of education and of charity, and the magnificent churches that beautify the City of New York.

Easily accessible, always "at home" to the humblest of his great flock, he was beloved by all. A sturdy American, he commanded the respect of men of all faiths. Among the thousands who dropped a tear at his bier were seen the Protestant minister, the Jewish rabbi, men high in all walks of life, and the lowliest of the poor.

The order has lost a good friend, the Church a noble son, the country a splendid citizen.

May his soul rest in peace.

The above resolution was adopted by rising vote at a meeting of the supreme officers of the Supreme Council, Catholic Knights of America, held May 31, 1902.

TELEGRAMS, LETTERS, AND
NEWSPAPER NOTICES

Santo Padre dolentissimo grave malattia cotesto Mgr Arcivescovo gli invia di cuore special Benedizione Apostolica.

M. CARD. RAMPOLLA.

ROME, April 26, 1902.

The Holy Father, very sorry for the dangerous sickness of the Archbishop, grants with all his heart special Apostolic Benediction.

M. CARD. RAMPOLLA.

Egregium Archiepiscopum quem summus Pontifex brevi visurum Romae sperabat, ereptum vivis esse maximo moerore cognovit. Sanctitas sua, quae praeclara defuncti, praesulis merita maximi aestimabat, Neo Eboracensi ecclesiae condolet exanimo et animae benemerenti Rmi Corrigan iustorum pacem et praemium ex corde adprecatur.

M. CARD. RAMPOLLA.

May 7, 1902.

The Holy Father with very deep sorrow has learned of the death of the eminent Archbishop, whom he had hoped to see very soon in Rome. His Holiness, who very highly appreciated the distinguished merits of the deceased prelate, sympathizes cordially with the Church of New York, and earnestly implores for the well-deserving soul of Archbishop Corrigan the peace and the reward of the just.

M. CARD. RAMPOLLA.

*The following has interest as the description of the Arch-
bishop's funeral by an outsider, Mr. Julian Hawthorne, in
the New York "American."*

DEAD on his bier lay the body of Michael Corrigan, a good
man, a zealous priest, an Archbishop of the Catholic Church.
He had risen from humble beginnings, and in little more
than sixty years he had become eminent in ecclesiastical
authority and honor. But he now lay dead on his high bier,
rigid and pale, with his hands, between which was a small
crucifix, crossed on his bosom. That, after all had been said
and done, was the central and most impressive feature of the
splendid ceremony performed yesterday.

The dead man was clad in his priestly vestments—the
princely purple, the high white mitre; the bier was richly
draped; around it burned a score of candles, shining in the
transparent gloom of the great cathedral like flowers of
soft fire.

He lay before the holy altar; upward on every side rose
the silent rows of fluted columns, draped to the carved
capitals in black; higher still was the delicate tracery of the
airy galleries; above them the broad windows glowing with
sacred scenes pictured in stained glass; and, surmounting all,
the fretted design of the arched roof.

The altar which rose behind him as he lay was rich with
harmonious decoration and twinkling with lights; and all the
elaborate splendor was strikingly contrasted with the cold
pallor of the enclosing walls of the edifice. Near by stood
the pulpit, graceful and imposing, with its great sounding-
board, on which was painted the Dove of the Church, seeming
to poise itself in air just above the head of the preacher.

It was, in its entirety, a solemn and glorious spectacle, well calculated to stir the most sluggish emotions. But the eminent priest lay quiet on his bier, unaffected by what moved all the living; for he was dead; his race was run and his work performed.

CHURCH CROWDED WITH SPECTATORS

THE church was filled to the walls with spectators, from whom arose a subdued sound of reverent talk and comment. Many of them had come from afar; they were old people and young, men and women (but women chiefly), rich and poor (but chiefly, it seemed, poor); Catholics and Protestants. Nor was the Hebrew race unrepresented; in a pew on the central aisle sat the Rabbi Gottheil, silent and absorbed. The civilized world is divided now, as it was in the beginning, between the Jews—the democrats—and the imperial Church of Christ.

The essence of what the one believes, the other, now as always, denies. But in these days, though the academic differences persist, the *odium theologicum* is subdued, and men of varying or hostile creeds meet as men and friends; the stoning of infidels and the inquisition on the heretics are no more.

The Church of Rome is the mightiest of all human organizations; it is substantial and perfect down to its last detail. From the central Christ of the creed, down through the Roman Pontiff, and so on, branching and disseminating from the red-capped cardinal to the humblest black-cassocked priest, the august and absolute spiritual authority is passed along, and exercised, and obeyed.

Every phrase used by the fathers in their speech with the faithful, in their prayers and addresses, in their ritual for every human and divine occasion, has been repeated since the earliest days of the Church; there is an endless vista of history and tradition behind them, giving them an awful weight and sanctity of influence and obligation; they possess something akin to a magical power; they are the refined and crystallized essence of the will of the Most High; the spiritual spontaneity which we cultivate in the dissenting churches is not countenanced in the ancient Church of Christ; in that Church, what has been, ever shall be, world without end.

CEREMONIES OF HOARIEST ANTIQUITY

Nor can we pause in our backward view of these wonderful ceremonies with the organization which dates from the early Christian centuries. Beyond them the tradition and the forms recede into an infinite perspective; pagan Greece and Rome and hoary Egypt, and those yet more remote religious exercises which we dimly trace in the records of Elam and the unknown East, have their contemporary representation in the Catholic solemnities of this twentieth century.

And over against these stand the not less antique and enduring beliefs of the great and mysterious Hebrew race, who believe in one unchangeable God, ancient of days, and who yet look for His Messiah. Before Him they stand in an unalterable and everlasting equality; the first of commonwealths, and possibly the last.

But they mingled yesterday with the others, and bowed their heads with them in harmonious respect to the memory of an honorable and worthy fellow-creature.

But the dead Archbishop lay motionless and undemonstrative on his bier and paid no heed either to Jew or Gentile, faithful or unfaithful. His interest in the things of earth was past forever.

After the hour at which the procession of priests was scheduled to appear there was a long interval of waiting, borne by the vast crowd in the pews more or less patiently; at times the organ sent forth its rolling melodies; candles burned; the sunlight fell through the tinted windows; the ushers moved on tiptoe to and fro; the closing of a pew door resounded through the hollow edifice.

The audience watched and waited, and the dead Archbishop also waited; all save waiting was over for him in this world, and there was no symptom of impatience from him. His hands that clasped the crucifix did not tremble; the expression on the sunken gray features did not change. Rigid and immovable he lay, waiting for what was to come; for the Day of Judgment and the last sound of the angelic trumpets.

THE AWFUL MAJESTY OF DEATH

To-day and to-morrow would pass away, and years would follow years, and the Archbishop would never stir hand or foot, or draw a laboring breath. He had entered into his rest, and none could disturb him again. He lay clad in his priestly garments and in the awful majesty of death.

At last, the wide doors in the front of the church were noiselessly thrown open and the blank, white daylight streamed in upon the columned obscurity. Thousands of heads were turned, and gradually the entire mass of human beings rose in their seats and looked toward the west.

The procession was about to enter. Slowly and with dignity they came, pacing two and two up the central aisle. Scores upon scores they passed, hundreds treading in the steps of hundreds; they walked with heads bowed and hands folded, the priests and dignitaries of the Church in their official vestments. Some wore on their shoulders surplices of white lawn or lace, others were clad in the severe garb of the monks; others appeared in plain black; still others, as the long file continued, showed the richer garments of the higher ecclesiastical orders.

Slowly and interminably they marched, defiling and deploying, passing up and onward until they were silently absorbed in the great space before the altar, behind and around the high bier with its august occupant. And still others came and others till the broad aisle was filled and the marchers paused and seated themselves, each man on the folding chair which had been provided for him.

It was a marvellous sight to see the profile of these priestly heads passing successively one after another, bowed and serious. Endless was the variety of types; inexhaustible the diversity of character; they were old and young, high and low, noble and plain, dignified and awkward, stern and mild, humble and proud, strong and weak; none was like another in all that multitude; and yet all had in common one look— the look of the Catholic priest—the look of mingled authority and obedience.

There is no other look that could be mistaken for it in the tribe of mortal men; it told of such a training and discipline as no other men are called on to sustain. It was the look worn by those who spread the doctrines of the Church over the face of the earth; who worked and suffered and died to save souls in the primeval wildernesses; who have built up in their fellow-men this mighty fact of the Catholic Church. It allied them one with another and brought them into unity, one stupendous organism, the body of Christ.

THEY constituted one of the greatest forces ever created on earth; quiet, subtle, omnipresent, well-nigh irresistible. Behind them lies a history of deeds unparalleled. And after two thousand years they seem as strong, as compact and purposeful as in the days of the early fathers.

These are the men who overthrew paganism, who rule to-day the larger part of the Christian world. From them emanated the holy army of martyrs and the company of the saints; from their ranks were chosen the popes who governed Europe and turned the tides of history. Their outward temporal power is no longer what it was; but the power of no temporal monarch equals theirs.

Authority and obedience mingle in their aspect; these are the virtues to which the world succumbs. Each as he passed the bier cast a glance upon him who lay there; but he gave no answering look. He had looked his last in the face of man; he was now facing a Countenance not mortal nor finite. He was dead, and immortally wedded henceforth to interests beyond the grave.

The long procession was stayed at last, and then ensued another interval, followed by the entrance of the Cardinal who was to officiate at the requiem mass. He came walking with feeble steps amidst a company of his brethren; on his head was the crimson beretta and he wore the red robes of his princely rank. His face was turned earthward; it was a worn and ascetic visage, scholarly and gentle.

Cardinal Gibbons is an older man than his fellow-priest who lay on the bier; but he still lived and the other had passed on to a life whereof the Cardinal knew nothing experimentally.

He, too, lifted his face as he went by the rigid figure outstretched yonder, and he bowed himself again in reverence to death. There came no answering obeisance; priestly rank had no further concern with Archbishop Corrigan, and had the Pope of Rome done homage to him he would have been met with the same silent and appalling indifference.

There is no respect of persons with God, and the Archbishop had been invested with a democratic dignity surpassing any that mortal authority can bestow. To death must we all come at last, and in the dust be equal made, and that equality is greater and more impressive than any nobility or royalty of living men. It endures forever.

Now preparation was made for the mass for the dead. Forgive thy servant, O Almighty One, for his sins; raise him up from the grave as Thy beloved Son was raised up! The organ pours forth its sublime notes and voices rise in music, praising and beseeching the Lord. At the high altar priest and acolyte perform their homage and deliver their ritual.

The candles shine in the holy dusk, the vestments gleam, there are bowings and prostrations, the plaintive voices of the worshippers implore the Unseen Power, the sweet, faint notes of bells sound from sacred recesses, the censers swing and the delicate precious perfume floats through the still air and dims with its light haze the adoring figures and the shrine at which they kneel.

Nothing done by man is more subtly moving in its influence than the Catholic mass; no other dramatic representation approaches it in significance and sublimity. It is the most wonderful and cogent appeal ever devised by humanity for the blessing and presence of its Creator.

After the plaintive implorings comes a hush. We seem to be looking far into the heart of a holiness and mystery too profound for speech or thought. Has the Most High indeed deigned to come down to us? Are we standing in that ineffable Presence? The silence sings in the waiting ear; then, of a sudden, with a glorious rush of sound, comes the organ thunder and the outburst of triumphant voices, shaking and overpowering the soul.

EMOTION STIRS ALL

THE Lord is with us; blessed be the name of the Lord! Who can withstand that marvellous outburst? What heart but must leap up and acknowledge that triumph? The audience vibrates with emotion; the priests avow their spiritual ecstasy; the atmosphere rocks with the storm of the acclaim; there is only one who remains unresponsive. That stern, meek figure on the bier is deaf even to this supreme appeal. His heart gives not a throb; his ears are deaf; he is dead in the midst of all this life and passion and uplifting of the soul.

Or is he rapt in a music compared with which this is but a discordant murmur? Do his closed eyes behold glories compared with which these are but as dust and ashes?

We cannot reach him; we cannot move him. What do we here in our darkness and impotence, thinking to honor him who is beyond all human honors?

The holy thunders of the mass die away and are stilled, and the Archbishop rests as before, inaccessible on his terrible throne.

Yet it was a spectacle and a ceremony well worth seeing, and to be taken deeply to heart. Doubtless those stern-visaged men, dressed in steeple-crowned hats and sad-colored garments, who came to us, when America was a wilderness, desiring to worship God in simplicity and freedom, doubtless these men would have looked strangely had they been told that their descendants after two hundred and fifty years would assemble in sympathetic thousands at such a celebration as this.

But the world moves and rises in each successive generation to a higher spiritual level and to a more complete comprehension of the brotherhood and companionship of man. The scene in the Catholic Church to-day is not a sign that we have fallen beneath the level of those stern forefathers of ours. It is a sign that humanity is becoming too great for the divisions of churches; that it is approaching a unity of all dissensions.

We have learned that God fulfils Himself in many ways, and that it is for Him and not for us to determine the manner of the fulfilment. The dead Archbishop on his bier rebukes all partisanship, and looking upon his pale, still countenance we may be prompted to compose our differences in favor of an accord which is so much wider and deeper than any difference.—JULIAN HAWTHORNE.

New York Tribune

IN the death of Archbishop Corrigan the American Roman Catholic Church loses, perhaps, its ablest administrator. As Archbishop of New York, without doubt the greatest office in the American Catholic Church, he was one of the most influential personages in the metropolis. He did not seem, however, to take a leading public part in general movements for the betterment of the community. As a result he was personally one of the least known of the city's eminent men to the general public outside of his own communion. But even if he had desired to take part in the larger civic life of the metropolis or nation, he would have found no time to do so, for the affairs of the archdiocese required his close and constant attention. He was, indeed, one of the busiest men in the city, and only succeeded in getting through the enormous mass of work laid upon his shoulders by his unwearied industry and system. In the administration of the archdiocese, representing, as it does, great and complex interests, he showed himself to be an able and firm ruler, who never for a moment allowed the reins to fall out of his hands. His winning personal traits greatly endeared him to those who came to know him well, and he had the respect and esteem not only of Catholics, but of Protestants, who saw in him a strong and unswerving churchman and a sagacious ruler.

To those who had the privilege of knowing Archbishop Corrigan personally he showed a side of his character that the general public did not suspect him of possessing. He was an accomplished scholar, especially in Church history and the classics, and a delightful conversationalist, with a keen though quiet sense of humor. He was a conservative churchman, but on terms of pleasant social intimacy with many who were not of his faith.

The New York Freeman's Journal

THE Catholic Church in America has lost by the death of Archbishop Corrigan one who for years has stood in the forefront in defence of Catholic interests in this country. Almost forty years a priest, twenty-nine years a bishop, and seventeen years an archbishop, the late Most Rev. Michael Augustine Corrigan spent his life in loyal service to the Church of which he was so devoted a son. Whether as Bishop of Newark or Archbishop of New York, he concentrated all his energies on the work he set his hand to.

The first Archbishop of New York was compelled to descend into the arena, and with pen and voice hold back the legions of bigotry which in the days of Know-Nothingism gathered to the assault. As we view, through the retrospect of the years, John Hughes unflinchingly facing the gathering storm, we instinctively exclaim, What a splendid protagonist! The work of the quiet, gentle-mannered Archbishop Corrigan lay in other fields. The more thorough organization of the archdiocese and the completion of the works begun by his predecessors in office was the task he set for himself—a task in the performance of which he never faltered for one moment till the hour that death struck him down. Churches, schools, convents, and especially the theological seminary that crowns the heights near Yonkers, will remain during the coming years as enduring monuments attesting to future generations the great work accomplished by the third Archbishop of New York.

When it is stated that in his archdiocese there are a million two hundred thousand Catholics whose spiritual wants have to be attended to, we can form an estimate of the magnitude of the labors that devolved upon Archbishop Corrigan. Never shirking them, he spent the last seventeen years of his life in laying deep and broad foundations on which his successors will be able to build. First and above all things a priest, he led a priestly life, and has left behind him a memory which will be held in veneration by those who had an opportunity of knowing his many virtues.

It was the knowledge of how richly he was endowed with these virtues that prompted Leo XIII to say, on hearing of his death: "It has been one of the greatest bitternesses of my long life to see the strongest champions of the militant Church claimed by death. Archbishop Corrigan was very affectionate towards us. We esteemed and loved him greatly." This eulogium shows how the Holy Father esteemed him for the work to which he devoted himself so zealously during life, and for which, let us hope, he will receive an eternal recompense.

New York American

THE great Church of which he was a distinguished prelate never had a more devoted servant than Michael Augustine Corrigan, Archbishop of New York. From early youth he was consecrated to the priesthood, and to its sacred duties he gave unstintedly all the powers of his life. He lived in and for the Church. His rare single-mindedness and exceptional abilities were early recognized at Rome.

Held in the deepest affection by Catholics everywhere, Archbishop Corrigan was universally respected. In his own diocese, where he was best known, men of all faiths and no faith revered him as an ardent Christian man and a most useful citizen.

Mourning for the dead prelate, therefore, is not confined to the Church which he loved so well and served so loyally. All, of whatever religious belief, who can appreciate the worth and dignity of a life given wholly to labor for the world's welfare, will pay the tribute of sorrow and esteem.

The Sun

ARCHBISHOP CORRIGAN has died in the prime of his career of thirty-nine years in the Roman Catholic priesthood. The scholarly bent and acquirement which had distinguished him even in his preparatory studies seemed to mark him out for a distinction which would be apart from the strenuous life of administrative and disciplinary activity upon which he entered with his appointment as Bishop of Newark in 1873. He was, moreover, of a slight and wiry physique, and of a disposition which was shrinking rather than aggressive. His vigor was rather in his head, in his intellect and his will, than in his body.

Archbishop Corrigan was distinguished by a repose and serenity both scholarly and of the cloister. His administration was firm and of a determined persistency, but it was without harshness, for he was naturally of a gentle and amiable disposition, and strife of itself had no attractions for him. His bearing was always marked by a priestly dignity which won for him the respect of a large social circle outside the ranks of Catholicism. In the pulpit he was a graceful, an earnest, and a persuasive speaker who appealed in simple and direct language to conviction rather than to the emotions.

The dead Archbishop was a religious figure entitled to respectful and even affectionate consideration from this community generally, even from people not of his own faith or of no religious faith at all. He lived to see the last traces of animosity to the Roman Catholic Church obliterated in every church, so that his death, on Monday, was looked on by all as a grievous loss to the cause of religion and good morals in New York. He left his archdiocese in a condition of greater prosperity and harmony than it had ever known throughout its history.

The Roman Catholics of New York were not suffered to enjoy the unmolested exercise of their religion until after the Evacuation of 1783. Then came and continued the suspicion and hostility which were inflamed into the passion of the Know-Nothing movement of the middle of the last century. But meantime the Catholics went on increasing steadily and rapidly, till now they are a vast communion, overshadowing in its magnitude all other churches. By the efforts of the dead Archbishop this great army of religion had been brought to a condition of disciplined compactness and unity notable in the history of the whole Roman Catholic Church.

The Mail and Express

THE death of Archbishop Corrigan falls as a heavy blow mainly upon the Church within whose ecclesiastical limits his whole world lay, but it is none the less a loss to the intellectual and religious life of the city and the State. His influence, direct and indirect, upon the multitude of those in his episcopal charge was felt by the entire community.

By temperament and training he was scholastic. He had none of the traits or tricks that win easy popularity. He became a master of men by mastery of mind. A conservative of conservatives, his life duty he deemed to be the preservation of the faith of his fathers. To that line he held inflexibly, viewing all innovations as encroachments upon the strength and safety of the Church. Beneath all the grace and modesty of a singularly sweet personality, his will was immovable.

Once convinced that a certain course of action was right and necessary, no argument and no influence could move him, save the command of his superiors, to whom he always gave the willing fealty that he demanded from his churchmen of lesser rank.

He was rich in ecclesiastical scholarship, in executive power, and financial ability, and his place in history is fixed among the great churchmen of America.

The Sunday Democrat

THE Most Rev. Michael A. Corrigan, Archbishop of New York, is dead. In those few words is recorded the great misfortune which has befallen the Catholic Church in America. Around that august and gentle figure of bishop and father the enthusiastic love of his children and his lovable character had already created an aureola of immortality. Every one avoided the sad thought that for him the last day in this '' vale of tears '' would come, the day when he would be compelled to leave his faithful priests and loving people and when he would fly from the cares and storms of terrestrial life to Paradise to receive his eternal reward. The great and solid merits of Archbishop Corrigan, to whom history and the Church will accord the rank which is his due, cannot well be over-' estimated. Of him it may be truly said that the copious grace of devotion poured out upon his flock showed how great was the piety and efficiency of his spiritual government.

Archbishop Corrigan's gentle kindness to visitors was remarkable. His good humor was apparent not merely in his kindly welcome of unwelcome visitors. It was seen in every trial of his life. He was never caught with a frown on his face. Nothing seemed able to ruffle him. Many instances might be given of this unfailing good humor. Where are we to seek the cause? Certainly not in the circumstances of his life. His day was one of almost uninterrupted toil. With the single exception of an occasional afternoon walk, he allowed himself no relaxation whatever. All day long he labored for his flock. A life like this might seem to tend to gloom. Yet he was ever bright and cheery. Where, then, shall we seek the cause of that lightness of heart which never seemed to desert him? The causes were, we think, two in number; one a negative and the other a positive cause. The negative cause was his humility. He was as humble in mind as he was in external life. He never sought himself, so he was never disappointed. The positive cause was his joy in his faith. And from the deep, intense joy which he found in it sprang that burning zeal for the conversion of his country which was the grand characteristic of his life as a Catholic. " Bonitas est diffusiva sui." He longed to communicate to others that perennial joy which the faith had given to himself. And to many hundreds he did, under God, communicate it. No priest or prelate was ever more humble, more conscientious, more self-denying than he. He lived for others, not for himself. " Pius, prudens, humilis, pudicus, sobriam duxit sine labe vitam "—these are the very words which best describe him. Every one knew Mgr. Corrigan, the Archbishop and scholar, but so retiring was he that few knew the man. We knew him well, and a man more indifferent to self we never knew. Who shall measure his work? Ask the priests, the prelates, and the people who wept at his bier. Ask the Great Judge and He will point to the churches, the parochial schools, and the grand seminary, and they will speak of it. But for him, the rest is silence. He has entered into a great peace.

The scenes at the Cathedral, while the body lay in state, were so many manifestations of respect for his memory and grief at his loss. People of all religions and many of no religion patiently waited their turn to take a last glance at the deceased prelate, and as they passed his bier few could restrain their tears. Rich and poor, Catholic and non-Catholic, gentle and simple, learned and unlearned, all alike paid tribute to the memory of the third Archbishop of New York. On every side one heard encomiums of his gentleness and charity. His " memory is an eternal benediction."

The Royal Prophet, rapt in the contemplation of future ages, may be said to have pronounced Archbishop Corrigan's praises in the beautiful words: " My truth and my mercy are with him." During the years of episcopacy we can see the reign of unbounded charity, unostentatious sanctity, and priestly zeal. For the past twenty-nine years his love of Christ appeared in its brightest colors and also his respect and affection for God's poor. Well might the poor weep over his bier and lament his loss. In the words of the sacred writer, " he was beloved of God and men." We are justified in applying to his life Cardinal Newman's description of " the round of days of many a pastor up and down Christendom; a life barren of great events and rich in small ones; a life of routine duties, of happy seclusion and inward peace; of an orderly dispensing of good to all who came within his influence morning and evening; of a growth and blossoming and bearing fruit in the house of God, and of a blessed death in the presence of his brethren."

The grand cathedral, now his last resting-place on earth, resounded with the dirge of death, and the hearts of those present beat in unison with the mournful cadences of the

" Dies Iræ." " Among holy things," says Schelling, " there is none holier than history, that great drama of the world— that everlasting poem of the Divine wisdom." And the future historian of the church in the United States will have no holier episode to relate than the obsequies of Archbishop Corrigan. The orator of the occasion, the Most Rev. Dr. Ryan, Archbishop of Philadelphia, justly applied to him the text, " He sanctified him in his faith and meekness and chose him out of all flesh ; . . . and placed a crown of gold upon his mitre, wherein was engraved holiness, an ornament of honor; a work of power, and delightful to the eyes for his beauty. . . . Therefore he made to him a covenant of peace, to be the prince of the sanctuary and of his people, that the dignity of priesthood should be to him and to his seed forever."

We would add that a full and true description of the funeral cannot be written. It is not given to human intelligence to gauge the depths of grief of the sorrowful congregation who were present at the obsequies. He was a grand figure in the American hierarchy, a bright star in the ecclesiastical firmament, and his loss was admirably painted in the truly eloquent sermon of Archbishop Ryan. To the world Archbishop Corrigan was a gentle and exalted dignitary of the Church, to his faithful priests he was a father and a friend. The recording angel has in " the book of life " the only full biography of the deceased prelate of the Church. And when that book is opened, and not till then, will mankind know the great services which he rendered to the United States and to the Church, of which he was such a distinguished ornament. From the day when His infant Church received her first baptism of fire, the Almighty has never ceased to pour out His Spirit on all flesh, but from time to time He chooses some who may receive these salutary streams, not for themselves alone, but for a posterity which lives on their spirit and finds therein a bond of social unity and a source of spiritual life and grace. And when this happens the grace of the Holy Ghost clothes itself with a particular outward form, puts on flesh and blood, and gives to each of these social bodies a tone and coloring of its own. And that this may not seem unworthy of the Spirit of God, it is enough to call to mind what St. Jerome says of the workings of the Holy Ghost in the Prophets. The same Spirit inspired them all. We may say of Archbishop Corrigan what the holy Doctor says of the speech of Isaias, " There was nothing vulgar about him, for he was a man of noble and gentle eloquence." When God called Archbishop Corrigan to the episcopacy He gave him all the graces and gifts necessary for his exalted station, and he faithfully co-operated with them. Hence his wonderful success in the Lord's vineyard. He was " a true shepherd," and his faithful flock lament his loss.

The Evening Post

THE sudden death of Archbishop Corrigan, who was supposed to be in the way to early recovery, is a heavy blow to the Church of which he was the local head. But it is something more than a cause of grief in the Roman Catholic communion. The Archbishop had made himself known to all New Yorkers, not merely as a type of the Christian walk and conversation, but as a man of nobility in every aim and endeavor that human life is capable of. He was a man who never did a thing or said a word for effect or to win applause. His way of serving his Master was unobtrusive, but his faithfulness to duty and his sweetness of disposition could not go without the reward of public recognition. So, when the twenty-fifth anniversary of his bishopric came to pass, there was a spontaneous demonstration of respect and admiration and affection from his fellow-citizens of all religious creeds—a demonstration which he received gratefully, but with the same quiet demeanor with which he would have received a visitation from the poorest members of his Church. Such a man leaves behind him a fragrant memory akin to that which, after seven hundred years, still clings to the name of St. Francis of Assisi.

The Evening Sun

A NOTABLE figure in our public life has passed away in the person of the Most Rev. Michael Augustine Corrigan, Archbishop of New York. The adherents of other creeds were interested in the personality of an ecclesiastic who carried on his shoulders for so many years the growing burdens of an archdiocese of such importance in the religious world.

In one of his early books, Cardinal Newman pointed out that there were two types of churchmen—those whose forte was administration, the workers, and those who in the seclusion of their studies and oratories lived the quiet life of scholars and theologians. One type was as necessary as the other as far as the welfare of the Church was concerned. The great figures among the early Fathers did not belong to either of these classes exclusively.

Dr. Corrigan was an able administrator. He had great initiative. His big archdiocese prospered under his care. To-day in the number of its churches, the flourishing condition of its charitable and educational institutions, it holds a distinguished place. A mere scholar would have found the load too heavy to bear. Hence, being a capable man of business, and of notable physical endurance, the late Archbishop was able to meet the responsibilities of his place. Throughout the period of his spiritual rule, the Roman Catholic Church in New York kept pace with the amazing material development of the community.

The New York Herald

Not only the Church of which he was so distinguished a prelate, but the city and the whole nation have sustained a loss in the death of Archbishop Corrigan.

By nature of a retiring and modest disposition, he seldom participated in public affairs outside his immediate ecclesiastical sphere, but when he did so his voice and influence were always to be found working for all that was best for the general good.

He was an exemplary ecclesiastic, reflecting the greatest honor on the metropolitan see over which he presided and the American branch of his Church. The number of new parishes he organized, the increase in the number of clergy, the impetus given to Catholic education, and the great diocesan seminary at Dunwoodie bear ample testimony to his zeal, and will be his most lasting memorials.

The Brooklyn Citizen

The death of Archbishop Corrigan leaves a gap in the religious field which the Church of which he was so sturdy an upholder will find it difficult to fill at once; for he was cast in a mould that seems to fit no other as yet well-known member of the priesthood of his time; and though all his great life work was done in and for the Church, it was naturally marked by his own strong and purposeful individuality, and carried out along lines that his knowledge and foresight assured of success.

He had all the zeal of the missionary, combined with the executive ability which enabled him to oversee the whole field of the work that was carried on under his direction; and the educational institutions established under his guidance, the increase in the number of the clergy and the organization of the many new parishes as well as the progress and solidification of the older ones, are all living memorials of his fitness for the high position he held in the Church.

The Albany Express

THE fact that the late Most Rev. Michael Augustine Corrigan was at the head of an archdiocese containing 220 parishes and more than a million communicants, was sufficient in itself to excite interest in the prelate's condition prior to his death. The director of the spiritual affairs of so many people must necessarily have been gifted with excellent judgment as well as untiring zeal in behalf of the interests which he represented to meet approbation at home and abroad.

Archbishop Corrigan was a brilliant, conservative prelate, and, as the head of the richest diocese in the world, exerted great influence in the Church. That he was a man of lovable nature was shown by the deep grief which thousands of persons of all denominations manifested upon the announcement of his death. His very important work was well performed.

He was a faithful servant of the Church, and in his exalted office was ever mindful of the strength and inspiration which come through reliance upon the Lord. May the good and true prelate's successor find inspiration in the noble life which has just ended!

The Albany Times-Union

By the death of Archbishop Corrigan the arrow of sorrow went home deep in the public heart. With friends, a host, and admirers, a multitude, but few men prominent in the public eye were as beloved and admired as was he. Power always brings fawners, always begets followers, but never produces the friends that stick through the thunders of opposition and the lightning shafts of disappointment, unless that power is tempered by justice, love, and mercy. These were the qualities that clothed Archbishop Corrigan's power and rule and made it always as attractive as the loadstone of a magnet, never repellant as princely sways sometimes become.

There is no aspect of Archbishop Corrigan's life that is not a monument to his memory and a credit to his Church. Broad of mind and liberal of heart, he ever conducted himself in his episcopate as an exponent of the theory that his Church is '' the mother of all the living,'' and as such never recreant to dry the tear of sorrow or allay the anguish, whether among the mightiest of the mighty, or the lowliest of the earth. As a man he was the pink of generosity, and while the benefactions of others may be blared from public trumpets or writ on marble columns, those of Archbishop Corrigan were given in accordance with the biblical injunction of '' let not thy left hand know what thy right hand doeth.'' He was meek of manner and kind of heart. '' Owe no man anything, but to love one another,'' was the motto of his career and the sermon of his life. The Golden Rule was with him the Alpha and the Omega of intercourse with fellow-men. His own church people loved him. Those of other churches admired and respected him. He always stood for the right and the true, and, though a lamb by nature, could rouse himself into a lion when battling for the cause of virtue, the triumph of right, and the reign of justice. The world is better for his having lived in it. He did untold deeds of good, and lies cold in death, with prayers ascending to heaven for him from thousands of grateful hearts.

To-day the Catholic Church of this archdiocese stands as once stood Rachel of old—weeping for her dead and refusing to be comforted, because he is not.

The Albany Argus

To all men, of whatever creed, the news of Archbishop Corrigan comes with a message of sadness. A distinguished and able prelate, his life of Christian usefulness and good deeds is all too soon cut off.

The Albany Journal

Sorrow because of the death of Archbishop Corrigan is not limited by creed. While the loss falls directly upon the great church organization in which he was a prelate, it is felt also by the public at large, for he was as distinguished and honored a representative of the citizens of the United States as he was of the Roman Catholic Church.

He took an active interest in all matters of public importance, and his influence was exerted for the promotion of the public welfare at every opportunity. He was broad and liberal in his views, and this quality, associated with a well-balanced combination of gentleness and firmness, gave him uncommon power over those that came under his influence.

His Church mourns him as a prelate; all Americans will mourn him as a loyal, progressive, esteemed fellow-citizen, as a friend of humanity.

The Newark Advertiser

IT is well observed by the " New York Evening Post " that the sudden death of Archbishop Corrigan is something more than a cause of grief in the Roman Catholic communion. As the " Post " truly says, the Archbishop was known, not merely as a type of the Christian walk and conversation, but " as a man of nobility in every aim and endeavor that human life is capable of. His way of serving his Master was unobtrusive, but his faithfulness to duty and his sweetness of disposition could not go without the reward of public recognition."

The " Post " adds that " such a man leaves behind him a fragrant memory akin to that which after seven hundred years still clings to the name of St. Francis of Assisi."

This noble tribute to a noble churchman is that of the great metropolitan spirit which judges all men according to their characters and works. The " Post " speaks the mind of every man who has observed the career of the late Archbishop, and can appreciate exalted qualities of character such as he possessed, qualities which raised him from a humble priest to one of the proudest positions in the prelacy of his Church. Had his career not been cut short by death, he would undoubtedly have received the red hat of the cardinalate.

The Philadelphia Press

No photograph or other counterfeit of Archbishop Corrigan's features was satisfactory or more than a remote resemblance to the face of this distinguished prelate. There was some quality of feature, of expression, some characteristic by which the Archbishop was peculiarly identified, especially to those who knew him best, which the camera could not catch and imprison, nor did any engraver ever master it by his art. The portrait-painter found the Archbishop's features not easy to reproduce in oil, while the characteristic expression, a singular combination of force and gentleness, seriousness, and kindly interest, the very quality which Matthew Arnold praised when he spoke of "sweetness and light," did not communicate itself to the painter's brush.

And this difficulty of transferring more than a remote likeness of the Archbishop's features to canvas or to print was also experienced by those who attempted an analysis of one of the most interesting, in many respects brilliant, profoundly intellectual, and yet peculiarly practical and forceful characters of his time, and one that has been of much influence and in a certain direction of pre-eminent authority and value in New York and, to some extent, in the entire country.

For Archbishop Corrigan's personality, not meaning by that his physical appearance, but the aggregate of intellect and temperament, was one which baffled analysis at times, or, at least, eluded analysis, excepting for those capable of study of that kind, and having abundant opportunity through an acquaintance and friendship maintained for many years with the Archbishop, which made possible a revelation of his many-sided character.

A peculiar distinction of Archbishop Corrigan's was that of seeming to be young always, and at the same time seeming always to be mature, and he was, in fact, apparently thus inconsistent. He was young in the freshness and vigor of his sentiments, in the innocence and purity of all his emotions, and in his appreciation of and fondness for the natural world around him, a disposition which he always kept thoroughly in check so that it would not master him. There was a sort of child-like innocence, simplicity, and lack of self-conscious-ness which contributed strongly to the impression of perma-nent youthfulness of nature which was always obtained by those who saw much of the Archbishop.

HIS KNOWLEDGE OF MEN

BUT, on the other hand, he was singularly mature, almost pre-cocious, even in his boyhood, not so much in respect to books or proficiency in school studies as in accuracy of judgment, a capacity to look upon life and its responsibilities and the rela-tions of men and women to the life about them as well as to the moral or higher life that indicated almost precocity, sometimes his instructors thought profundity, of thought. And this quality remained with the Archbishop throughout his life, so that friends, especially those who met him in the social life that he graced and in the companionship where he felt free from restraint, were sometimes amazed by listening to brief but very lucid, clear, and often profound comments upon the greater affairs of this world, the intellectual character of men who had achieved or were achieving, while at the same time these comments were made in an almost diffident way, but not exactly diffident, either, for the Archbishop was utterly without self-consciousness, but in a modest, suggestive way without any self-assertion, almost as an inquiry.

The freshness and purity of his outlook and understanding were tempered, too, by a keen sense of humor that might easily have enabled the Archbishop to acquire the reputation of a wit; for he had a gift of concise utterance and for the likening of unlike things in an unexpected manner, which is the soul of wit. But he knew that wit was a dangerous gift, and in a prelate of his standing, even although scrupulously guarded, might degenerate into something undignified, something that would occasion a wound. Therefore, while his personal conversation was often rich in gentle and kindly humorous suggestion, he never allowed it to culminate into witty expression.

A YOUNG PRELATE

He came to the great see of which New York is the centre, and which includes the Bahama Islands as well as much of the territory that is contiguous to New York, when he was still a very young man in years, but mature in experience, in intellectual qualities, and, singularly, unexpectedly mature in gifts of executive direction, gifts that brought to him tributes of admiration from the men of greater affairs of New York, with whom he was often brought into contact in connection with the business administration of his archdiocese. He died, too, before he became venerable in years, for he was still a young man, as the age of youth in the greater business or professional affairs is esteemed. But he had achieved in the seventeen years of his administration as archbishop results that could not have been reasonably expected in an administration of twice the length of his own.

His executive capacity and performance may be traced to a remarkable power of concentration, a gift for economizing and systematizing time, an ability to direct those who carry out details and to himself administer to the utmost detail. Had his vocation been that of business, he would easily have taken place among the organizers of great forces and among the directors of them, but it would not have been through any impressive physical demonstration. He did not have the fiery personal and physical characteristics of one of his distinguished predecessors, John Hughes, who was a mighty force in this city and in the nation at the time of the Civil War, who could be splendid in worthy passion and righteous indignation and at times, too, when those qualities were necessary.

Archbishop Corrigan's achievement as a business leader would have been compassed partly by sheer intellectual force, partly by consummate tact, of which no man of New York was ever greater master, and partly by a singular power of gentle persuasion, which would, had he been a politician, have made him a masterly one.

HIS SPIRITUAL LIFE

He had mastered whatever weaknesses of his nature there ever were, so that he was completely dominated by spiritual force and impulse. And when an example was sought in this city so that the power of spiritual communion, of piety, of religious, as distinguished from moral, influence to dominate the whole character, intellectual and temperamental, of a man, Archbishop Corrigan received that tribute. Others have been of saintly character, as was his immediate predecessor, Cardinal McCloskey, but Archbishop Corrigan was of that quality, while at the same time maintaining often physically excessive and always exacting administrative and executive relations with the diocese, which upon its business side had become not only a great financial, but a great co-operative community. As a financier—and he had much of that employment, especially in connection with St. Patrick's Cathedral, and with the endowments of the many charities and philanthropies which were under his direction, as well as the finances of the Church, which were in the aggregate very large—his judgment was always keen and seemed to act intuitively. The able bankers like Kelly and Crimmins and Grace, who, as laymen, were often associated with him as advisers upon the financial undertakings of his diocese, learned not only to respect his judgment and to have confidence in it, but to look to him for the initiative.

In some respects the financial administration of such a see as that over which Archbishop Corrigan was in authority is as comprehensive, as delicate and detailed, and, in the amounts of money involved, as large as is that of some of our larger banking institutions. And when to this it is added that he was the administrative as well as the religious authority over institutions numbering in their membership nearly 70,000 persons, dependent upon philanthropy or charity, or upon the gentle, corrective discipline of the Church, it will be seen that here was a veritable army of itself, of which he was the head, and which, nevertheless, was only a small division of that army, great in numbers and in influence, which represented the whole of his archdiocese. From this there will be some understanding of the purely administrative qualifications that are demanded of him who successfully directs as great affairs as these.

AND yet this was only one side of this brilliantly complicated character. The Archbishop was able to turn, after a day's labor at the archiepiscopal residence, not to lighter, but to different things, and to become on the instant the profound scholar, the real academician. The breadth of his cultivation and the cosmopolitan character of his learning may be illustrated by an incident that occurred last summer. The Archbishop was taking his recreation in the late afternoon, as he was fond of doing, by a stroll upon Fifth Avenue. He liked the animation, the brilliant moving picture, the health and activity that are displayed at that hour of the day anywhere from Twenty-third Street and Fiftieth Street, a stretch of a mile and a half. If he was a conspicuous figure upon the avenue, it was not by reason of any posing or affectation. He was conventional in his dress, and to a stranger would have seemed no more than any one of the well, though modestly, dressed pedestrians; but he was so well known, he was of such high authority, his influence had been of such pre-eminent value, especially at one time of dangerous crisis, that he was a conspicuous object—more conspicuous than he himself ever realized. He met one day last summer, as he was turning at Twenty-third Street to return, an humble parishioner, a Frenchman, teacher in a private school, a man of learning and of fine character, but who had always struggled for a livelihood, and the Archbishop invited this teacher to walk back with him, saying, " I fear I am a little rusty with my French, and if it will be agreeable to you I should like to talk with you in French as we stroll back." And there began then a conversation in the French language carried on by the Archbishop without hesitation, with only the slightest foreign accent, and it was a conversation upon French literature, especially the classics, and the tendency, demoralizing, as the Archbishop thought, of the later literature of France.

Had the Archbishop been a professor of letters he could not have discussed these questions with greater clearness or profounder understanding than he did upon this occasion. And if upon that same stroll he had met an Italian friend he would have been able to converse with him as easily in the Italian language as he did to the French professor in the language of France. Of course, he read Hebrew and Greek, and was proficient in Latin—proficient both as a reader of the language and in ability to converse in it. He had, too, as one of his recreations,—singular amusement for the relaxing of a busy brain,—a fondness for mathematics, and especially for astronomy. In addition to these cultivated tastes, the Archbishop was a keen observer of the greater influences that are making American life what it is. In no sense a partisan, he recognized the need of parties in a Republican-Democratic form of government, and he was an eminently just judge both of principles and of policies. He was fond of saying that upon the fundamental principles which are the basis of our form of government the two great parties do not disagree, but only upon the policy, the expedient way of putting those principles into force. He did discover a tendency to depart from moral principles in some of our more recent political agitations, and it gave him great pain, but he had firm faith in the overwhelming moral sense of the American people, and in their capacity on the whole, and in the long run, to act wisely, justly, and in accordance with the moral law.

ELISHA JAY EDWARDS, LL.D.

The Utica Observer

ARCHBISHOP CORRIGAN's career as administrator of the great see of which New York is the centre, and whose authority extended as far away as the Bahama Islands, was ended by death at a comparatively early age. He was, at the time of his death, but little older than his predecessor, the saintly McCloskey—who was elevated from the archbishopric of New York to a cardinalate—was when he entered upon his administrative duties in this archdiocese. Archbishop Corrigan was nearly ten years younger at the time of his death than the age at which Archbishop Hughes passed away, after an administration of this diocese in one of the stormiest of times. But Michael Augustine Corrigan was always a mature—and, in his boyhood, almost a precocious—person. In his childhood he was serious, contemplative, studious, and was deemed both by his teachers and by his boy associates to be, as the saying is, " beyond his years." The same quality distinguished him when he was passing through the university, and also when engaged in his theological and sacred studies. Of him it can be said with perfect truthfulness that, although his intellect ripened early, his intuitions were so great and his capacities so profound that he was able to pass any instant, while still a young man in years, on the threshold of a career, from the academy to the professor's chair, to the administration of one of the most important bishoprics of his Church in the United States.

The facts that outlined the career of Archbishop Corrigan as the public saw it have already been published; and there has been appropriate, sympathetic, and most adequate comment in the newspaper press upon the character and achievements of this distinguished prelate. But it may be of interest to set forth briefly the more subtle qualifications, intellectual and moral, of Archbishop Corrigan, as they were discovered by those who were privileged to have a closer intimacy with him than was possible for any who came in contact with his personality in no other way than through the administration of his ecclesiastical or his executive functions. In temperament, the Archbishop was a singularly happy combination of those qualities which produce perfect serenity, even poise, tact, and a kindly, gracious approach and communication with his fellow-men. He was blessed with a very keen sense of humor and, within proper limitations, he allowed it full play. For this reason he was, in his moments of leisure and on those delightful occasions of social intercourse which he too seldom permitted himself, one of the most charming of story-tellers; and he had a fund of anecdotes, tinged with gentle, delightful humor, sometimes with harmless, gentle satire, that, as he spoke, reminded those of his hearers who had been readers of the style and manner of Charles Lamb. If he had great passions, he had thoroughly conquered them in his early life. He could be indignant, even earnest and passionate, but only against wrongs or harmful tendencies, never against individuals. It was probably easier for him than it would have been for many men to preserve this equableness of temper, since it was a native quality, not needing much discipline to maintain; but if discipline had been required, it would have been self-administered, for of all the citizens of New York of his day and generation, none had his faculties, his emotions, his passions under such complete subjugation to his will and to the sublime purpose which actuated his life, to a greater degree than Archbishop Corrigan.

His temperament was of the character that enabled him to obtain the highest results from his intellectual and his executive qualifications. His was an unusual combination of very great executive ability with very profound powers of reasoning, in the abstract as well as the concrete, with capacity to absorb, perfectly to digest and assimilate learning; so that he might one day be found devoted to the vocations of a scholar, pure and simple, and on the next be wholly occupied with the tremendous energies, with the swift and accurate judgment, and the skilful use of authority which the business administration of the vast machinery of the archdiocese of which he was the head required. In this respect Archbishop Corrigan was peculiarly distinguished from his two immediate predecessors, Cardinal McCloskey and Archbishop Hughes.

Archbishop Corrigan was one of the most saintly of men. But his archdiocese had grown so enormously, it required such constant and excessive employment of executive faculties, even for the purely business administration of it—an administration that involved the handling of very large amounts of money, the wise direction of great landed or other properties, the administration of estates and trusts, as well as the oversight of many clergymen and authority exercised over the bishops—that the remarkable business and executive qualifications Archbishop Corrigan displayed were, with business men, more apt to cause striking and impressive measurements of the Archbishop's qualities, than did the saintly or scholarly character which was really even more fully developed than his executive and business capacity. It is an unusual combination. We have had a saintly administrator, preeminently and conspicuously of that quality, and we have had a statesmanlike, aggressive, and wise business administrator;

but I think it is safe to say that we have never had, until Archbishop Corrigan, in one person, an even balance between both of these qualities developed to a very high degree. It was only to a few that his real scholarship was revealed, for he was the most unpretentious, modest, and unassuming of men. He prized learning, both for its own sake and for its discipline of the mind and the experience which it gave. But he was never pedantic. Some of his accomplishments were those of men of the highest cultivation, as, for instance, he spoke French with perfect facility, as he did Italian, although his acquirement of Italian came in the natural course of things, since he was a student for several years at the American College established in Rome. He learned French outside of the personal environment which he had at Rome. He was a profound Hebrew and Greek scholar, and, of course, was a master of the Latin tongue. He was, too, intensely interested in the great material achievements of his day, having no narrow, scholastic, or closet-like contemplation of the great world in which he lived, and it was no doubt in part due to this tendency, as well as to his profound understanding of the philosophy and ethics as well as the vital teachings of his Church, that led him to take the conspicuous stand he did, and one which will always be associated in the mind of the public of New York with his career of archbishop.

Archbishop Corrigan, in his relations as a citizen, was a very profound believer in the influence for good of American institutions. He knew the strength and the weakness of our people, of our laws, of our public opinion. He was singularly lucid and rational in his analysis of great popular movements. He never, of course, took any part in purely partisan politics. He recognized that in both of the great parties there was much

of good and some of evil, and that both together represented
the American people. He easily separated the vital from the
unimportant; and while there was never any tolerance on his
part for any partisan or political action that involved what
he believed to be a breach of the moral law, there was, on the
other hand, the greatest tolerance for difference of opinion
upon matters that were purely questions of expediency or of
policy. While one of the foremost and truest and most loyal
and conscientious of the supporters of the doctrine and authority of the Church he so nobly represented, he was nevertheless
no bigot, and welcomed in all philanthropies, in all great moral
works, the support of people of every denomination. Archbishop Corrigan was a very great man in intellect, in executive
force, and in the perfect and absolute subordination of his
qualities of temperament and of intellect to his vocation and
to his duties. He was a great man intellectually; and he had
the modesty of true greatness, seeming at times almost shy.
His death is a great loss to New York, a keen bereavement to a
vast circle of friends, both in and out of his Church; and his
name will be honored and become a tradition, not only within
the circle of his Church and of his important authority in the
Church, but also throughout this community.

> " In the great Cathedral leave him ;
> Christ accept, and God receive him."

THOMAS L. JAMES.

The Buffalo Courier

HARDLY was the public prepared for the intelligence that Archbishop Corrigan died late Monday night, for it had seemed
that the crisis of his illness had favorably passed, that the

prayers of all of his faith, the wishes of his countrymen of whatever faith, were to be satisfied. But the peaceful rest which stimulated hope for his recovery was to merge quickly into the rest eternal. His labors were finished and he went to his reward. The decease of this prelate is an event of sorrowful interest to the Christian world, for few in a field so great have performed so vast a temporal as well as spiritual work, increasing the tangible agencies of religion by the creation of churches, schools, and institutions of benevolence which veritably are a multitude.

Michael Augustine Corrigan was an appreciative, patriotic citizen of the United States, ever regardful of the welfare and jealous of the honor of the land of his birth. While his life labor was primarily for the advancement of religion, he ever conducted himself to furnish an example in good citizenship. Of his rapid and brilliant rise in ecclesiastical position and influence it is not needful to repeat the details here.

The Archbishop was a splendid combination of moral, mental, and physical force. As there are captains of industry in our modern business life, so was he a captain of religion in America. His work was enormous, its results beneficent and enduring. '' Precious in the sight of the Lord is the death of His saints.''

The Providence Telegram

Most Rev. Michael Augustine Corrigan, D.D., Archbishop of New York, whose death occurred at the episcopal residence in New York City last night, was one of the foremost prelates in the United States. He was rated with the first-grade scholars of the Catholic Church in America, and was renowned for his piety, zeal, and self-sacrificing efforts in the line of his duty. The Archbishop was not an old man, as churchmen go, being but sixty-two. He had lived the strenuous life, but his labors had been strictly in the line of, closely in harmony with, the duties of his sacred calling. Unlike some other noted prelates, Archbishop Corrigan never mingled in politics; his life work was in the Church, which had honored him and which he had honored.

To the Church, which he loved, was given his every thought, and in its service he expended his energies with no care for the hardships to self. In fact, self-effacement was the key-note of his priestly character. His flock had his constant care, and the growth of his archdiocese is the best monument to his memory.

The Buffalo Times

THE predictions of the physicians of Archbishop Corrigan, as announced in " The Times " of yesterday, have been sadly verified, and the distinguished prelate breathed his last shortly after 11 o'clock last evening.

Archbishop Corrigan was a man of extraordinary educational attainments, of loving and affectionate nature, broad-minded and generous; loved and reverenced by his own Church, and held in the highest esteem by others. He was essentially the right man for the position which he filled, and his death has created a grievous loss, which will not easily be replaced.